MAYA

IN

MANHATTAN

Anita Rani

iUniverse, Inc.
New York   Bloomington

Maya in Manhattan

iUniverse books may be ordered through booksellers or by contacting:
iUniverse
1663 Liberty Drive
Bloomington, IN 47403
www.iuniverse.com
1-800-Authors (1-800-288-4677)

ISBN: 978-1-4401-3219-3 (sc)
ISBN: 978-1-4401-3220-9 (e-book)

Printed in the United States of America

iUniverse rev. date: 04/7/2009

CHAPTER 1

"I got the job?" Maya said excitedly with the phone hugging close to her right ear and a half-eaten apple held in her left hand.

"Yes, that is correct. We will be sponsoring you for a work permit, so your start date will be as soon as the visa is approved. Congratulations, Miss Jain, your offer letter will be mailed to you today, and we look forward to having you onboard," responded the recruiter on the other end in a polished voice.

Maya dropped the phone and looked at her best friend, Renee, who had stopped by after a long day at the hospital.

"Oh my god, Renee, I am moving to Manhattan! Yippee!" Maya hugged Renee tightly with a sparkle in her eye.

"That's crazy. Why would you want to move to Manhattan when all your friends are here?"

"Well, for one thing, think of all the good-looking guys in Manhattan. Millions of them! This is the chance to meet the man of my dreams. And besides, you know I have some good friends down there. Remember Toni? She is so cool and has an amazing job at a prestigious law firm. I am sure she will introduce me to her friends. I'll be meeting a lot of people."

"I'm so happy for you, Maya. But I will miss you. You're like the sister I never had," Renee responded. She and Maya had developed a very close friendship over the past seven years.

"I will miss you too and all of my friends. But, this is Manhattan. There's not a city in the world like it. And I have the chance to experience the Big Apple. Yeah!" Maya did a little jig with a twinkle in her eyes and grabbed Renee's arms, dancing with her in a circle.

Later that night, Maya recalled the recruiter's words, which echoed in her mind. "Yes, we are interested in hiring you." Was this is a dream or had she really been offered a new job — a new life — in the Big Apple? Was she finally going to find love? There were millions of single men in Manhattan, and so the odds definitely looked good! Hope springs eternal, and to Maya the offer was a godsend; this was the event that had the potential to change her entire life.

Maya was thirty-one years old and had lived in downtown Toronto for the past seven years. She came from Charlottetown, Prince Edward Island, a small town situated in the Gulf of St. Lawrence on the eastern coast of Canada. Maya had distinct memories of her beautiful Canadian mother, Natasha, a fiery redhead whose stunning green eyes combined with her voluptuous figure easily caught a male eye, and her much older but very young-at-heart Indian father, Raj Jain. Raj was an endearing, soft-spoken man, blessed with a quick smile and an equally quick wit. He had arrived in Charlottetown to study mechanical engineering in the seventies, and met Natasha while he was a graduate student in his mid-twenties, while she was in her first year of college.

Raj and Natasha married out of physical attraction and sheer idealistic love. After a three-year courtship, the desire for stability and raising a family had spurred Raj to propose. And so they had married; however, over time, the two had fallen out of love when the demands of real life had set in. They varied greatly in their values, and both were stubborn and unyielding on larger elements of life, such as caring for extended family members. Financial burdens and strains had eventually driven them apart. Maya had memories of her mother yelling at her father many a time, and specifically, she recalled a bitter fight when Raj had sent over fifteen thousand dollars to his sister and parents in India. Natasha claimed that left nothing, only bare necessities for both her and Maya. The final blow to their marriage occurred when Raj was laid off from the small engineering firm that had employed him for seven years. The company had collapsed in a weak economy, and it had taken Raj six months to find another job. Neither could see eye-to-eye on their finances. Natasha had little sympathy for his situation, as she herself had stopped working when Maya was born and was accustomed to living a certain lifestyle. She had thrown a fit in response and subsequently took off for a two-week vacation to a small villa in Florence, leaving Maya alone with her dad.

In Tuscany, Natasha met and fell in love with a young Italian gentleman. He was a successful art dealer with a burgeoning business across the Atlantic. Their attraction for each other was instant and neither had resisted the temptation to indulge in the affair. The Italian art dealer, Giuseppe, moved to Atlantic Canada after six months of love letters and phone conversations with Natasha. Thus, Maya's parents divorced when she was ten years old, and although she had been too young to understand what was happening, the raised voices and accusations between her mother and father had made her feel like she was splitting in two, as if someone was brutally pulling apart her organs, one by one. As an only child, Maya couldn't find comfort in the arms of any siblings; rather, her loneliness at home made her shy and withdrawn, which resulted in very few friends at school. After the divorce, Maya lived at home with Natasha in their three-bedroom house, which Raj had vacated shortly after her mother's announcement of her affair. The Italian art dealer had moved in and although he was very polite to Maya, he paid little attention to her, parading around, often bare-chested with a cigarette dangling from his mouth. As a result, Maya often felt ignored, as her mother had been, for the most part, focused on pleasing her new boyfriend, Giuseppe.

On alternate weekends, Maya would visit her father across the harbor in his small two-bedroom condo, which had been home after the divorce. The fact that her parents were divorced didn't stop Maya from secretly hoping that her parents would realize their mistake and would soon reconcile, becoming a family again. It took a long time before Maya realized that her hopes were fruitless. Natasha ended up marrying the Italian art dealer. Maya never truly warmed up to him, and he could not supplant the father she knew and loved. Maya looked forward to spending alternate weekends with Raj, who was focused on spending quality time with her. He amused and entertained her as best as he could. He would often arrange play dates with other single fathers in the community who had children close to Maya's age. They would have pool parties at the condominium complex where he lived and often hosted friends for the day. They also went to amusement parks together and Raj was a very protective father, as his only daughter, Maya, was the apple of his eye.

When Maya turned thirteen, Raj remarried an Indian woman named Sheela who had never been married, nor did she have any kids of her own. Maya remembered the first time her dad spoke to her about his new love, and the same feelings of hurt and confusion quickly came back to her, as when she had been first told about her parents' separation. Raj did his best to explain his new romance as gently as he could. He told Maya that he felt connected to Sheela, that she was a good woman, nurturing and warm, and he felt that she would stand by him, both in good and hard times. Maya was surprised when she met Sheela for the first time. She was stricken by her stepmother's youthfulness, her dark Indian beauty and her warm, easy manner. Sheela was pure Indian, although she had grown up in Canada. She seemed genuinely interested in Maya, and it was very apparent to Maya how much she loved her father. But Maya was very stiff for the first several meetings with Sheela, as she resented this woman who had replaced her mother as her dad's new wife. It took a while before Maya warmed up to Sheela. How could she accept that her parents were no longer together and now this other woman was to be the object of her dad's affection? Would her father still want to spend time with her? However, Raj was sensitive to his daughter's confusion and hurt, and never sacrificed his time with Maya. After a few months, thanks to his and Sheela's genuine efforts to engage Maya, she began a friendship with Sheela, which would soon become a strong, enduring bond.

Maya was exposed minimally to the Indian culture while growing up, having been brought up on macaroni and cheese and peanut-butter sandwiches. It was a pleasant culinary change when weekend dinners at her father's had become purely home-cooked Indian meals with the scents of curry spices filling the air at dinner time. Sheela cooked very simple but tasty dishes, such as daal, rice and a vegetable, such as potatoes or okra. Maya slowly acquired the taste of Indian food, and eventually looked forward to the dishes prepared by Sheela. Sheela was also a very fashionable woman who enjoyed going to Indian concerts. Maya recalled the time when Raj and Sheela took Maya to Toronto for a big Indian Bollywood concert where all of the dancers, actors and actresses on stage had been flown in from Mumbai to perform. The danseuses were ordained with large, gold exquisite jewelry and heavily embroidered, gorgeous saris.

The dance performances were nothing like Maya had ever seen, and she was awed by these Indian beauties on stage who danced so perfectly and with such grace. She loved the performance and after a while, Maya genuinely became fond of Sheela and began to embrace the culture that was also her own. She began to look up to Sheela as a role model, and she was always awed by her dark beauty and warm nature. Maya started to confide in Sheela about her crushes on boys at school. Maya never told her own mother about her blossoming relationship with Sheela, as she knew that Natasha would disapprove, and she wouldn't have hurt her mom for the world.

By her sixteenth birthday, Maya had blossomed into a beautiful, shy young woman who maintained an unassuming profile amongst her peers. Her awkward stage had passed and the most noticeable change in her appearance was her curvaceous figure, which drew many second looks from normal, healthy males. It was her last year in high school and she was looking forward to the fall when she would start her first year of college. It was during that summer that Maya experienced her first serious crush. He was a college exchange student and two years her senior. His name was Bruce and he was a lanky average-height lad who had sandy-brown hair and light freckles on his face. He also had blue-green eyes, and Maya met him at the bookstore of the local college campus where she was purchasing textbooks for her first year of college. She was waiting in line to pay for them and Bruce was behind her; when he caught her looking back, he had immediately struck up a conversation with her.

"Hi there. What's your name?" he said with a very interested look in his eye, and an accent that she could not place.

"Maya," she responded and smiled politely.

"Hi, I'm Bruce. Are you from this town? It's my first time in Charlottetown. I'm an exchange student from New Zealand and just here for the summer to study French."

"Wow, I've never met anyone from there. What's it like down there?" Maya responded.

"It's awesome. Why don't I tell you over coffee tonight? Bruce responded flirtatiously.

And that was the start of Maya's first romance with a boy. The same night they met, Maya and Bruce hung out at a local downtown bar, and after a few drinks, Bruce took her back to his dorm room. He didn't waste any time and Maya was also starving for physical affection. She was sixteen and a virgin, and her hormones were on fire. She passionately kissed Bruce for what seemed like hours, and welcomed his advances eagerly. He lifted her blouse to cup her full breasts and tugged on her nipples. They became firm instantaneously and he immediately placed his hands underneath her underwear. Before long, both were naked and while he was on top, he drove into her repeatedly, with furious pleasure, for the next several hours. Maya's pain was sharp the first time Bruce entered her, but the second was less so, and it wasn't long before Maya started to experience her own sweet pleasure and craved for his sexy, lean body.

For the rest of the summer, Maya and Bruce were inseparable. Their passion for each other intensified and

Maya escaped to be with him, as time would permit between his French lessons and her family commitments. He was her first love, but as with most teenage romances, the ending was too close and the day for Bruce to return back to his hometown in Auckland came sooner than later. Promises to write and visit were made, but both knew it would be difficult to keep up a relationship. Bruce's departure shattered Maya's young heart and she felt intense sorrow for months, as he had been her first serious infatuation. However, the reality of school set in very quickly and she soon became very busy with her classes and making new friends. Maya was a good student and focused intently on her studies to achieve the high grades her father aspired for her.

Maya's four years in college flew by and after graduating summa cum laude with a Bachelor's degree in business, followed by a Master's in business, she was ready to spread her wings and fly to the melting pot of Toronto, known as the cosmopolitan centre of Canada.

Her years in Toronto were a blast. She was twenty-four years old and was working as a junior banker with normal nine-to-five hours, and finally earning some decent money. It was a relief to no longer have the pressure of school and grades, and to deal with her father's huge expectations of her. Although she loved and respected him, she had felt a tremendous amount of pressure to excel in all of her subjects. Thank goodness she had done well and passed with honors in most of her courses. Maya rented a two-bedroom apartment in downtown Toronto near Queen's Park, and it was a stroke of luck that she ended up rooming with a girl who would become one of her closest friends. Rita was a ball of fire; she had an endless amount of energy and was utterly confident in herself. Her interests were diverse; she loved sports, debating, traveling and concerts. Maya had never met anyone like her. Rita drew her out and together they went to parties, traveled to Europe and the Caribbean and even went out on double dates. On one New Year's Eve, the two of them had attended three different parties throughout the night, and when they reached back home at sunrise on New Year's Day, both girls were so inebriated that neither was able to open their eyes until midday. The partying was fun, the recovery a bit brutal, but both girls had a blast, taking on Toronto and enjoying its nightlife together.

Rita's energy was contagious, and she influenced Maya greatly to shed her shyness so that Maya eventually became a vivacious, outgoing and adventurous young woman.

Maya formed many close friends in Toronto and her social life was a whirlwind, full of fun and warm memories. Her closest friends included Renee, who was a physician by trade and had a heart of gold, and Ida, whom she had clicked with instantly as they shared the same sense of humor. The years passed quickly and things also changed in time. Rita moved on to take a job south of the border, in Pennsylvania, with a big pharmaceutical firm, and a few of Maya's close friends had moved to the Big Apple to pursue their careers. Maya was thirty-one years old and seven years later, when the thrill of her life in Toronto dimmed, she herself welcomed the opportunity to move on. The new job she had been offered was a godsend and she was now more than ready to take on Manhattan.

Chapter 2

The smell of warm roasted peanuts filled the air, as Maya crossed Central Park to arrive at the North-Americas headquarters of Bearings Bank, which was a blue-blooded 150-year-old British investment bank. It was December 11, 1997, and it was her first day on the job in Manhattan on Park Avenue. As she entered the large brass doors of Bearings Bank, she felt like a million dollars. Never in her wildest dreams had she ever dreamed of having a Park Avenue address and a cool apartment on Broadway in the heart of the Upper West Side.

Her boss, Charlie, greeted her in a deep husky voice, "Hello Miss Jain." The other members of the team were rather an odd bunch. There were four men in total, two of which were bean pods (accountants, that is) and an older man (he looked like he should have retired several years back), and a middle-aged man with thick dark glasses who spoke in a heavy, Brooklyn accent. The group secretary was an older woman named Linda who appeared to be a very fashion-conscious Italian woman. Maya specifically liked the hairdo, which was reminiscent of a Greta Garbo type look. It was a very diverse and eclectic group. Linda and Maya would soon become fast friends and Maya learned to respect Charlie immensely. He had a photographic memory and could recall every single detail of his clients' backgrounds and their financial situations.

After a long day at work, Maya walked through Central Park to her new doorman apartment at the corner of 72nd and Broadway. While crossing the street towards her apartment, she felt a tap on her shoulder, and turning around was surprised to see a young boy who looked no more than ten years old, wearing a torn shirt. It was clear he was homeless, and he looked up at her and waved a twenty-dollar bill at her.

"You dropped this," he said, looking up at her with his big eyes.

Maya was stunned. It was hard to believe that a homeless boy in Manhattan was actually giving her back the twenty-dollar bill she had accidentally dropped. She immediately felt touched and smiled at him. "Please keep it. It's yours now," she said and continued walking towards her building.

The doorman greeted her with a warm smile. He was taken by Maya's beautiful angular jaw, high cheekbones and almond eyes of this slender, petite girl whose olive skin appeared tanned and flawless, like someone who had just flown in from the Mediterranean. She was also full breasted and because she was petite, she had a curvaceous figure that often drew the attention of a man's second look.

Maya stepped into her twenty-first-floor apartment and looked around, absorbing the small spatial configurations and her furniture. She thought she had done a fairly decent job of furnishing the place, although on a budget. *Thank god for Ikea*, she thought. Manhattan apartments were ridiculously expensive and the monthly rent easily took one half of her monthly salary. The phone rang. "Hello." The familiar voice answered on the other line; it was her best friend in New York, Toni, who had also been her former roommate in Toronto.

"There is a really cool party tonight; it starts at ten o'clock and is a charity event for Alzheimer's. And it's at the Manhattan penthouse. There should be a lot of cool guys there." *Wow, Toni works really fast*, thought Maya. She had only been in the city for a week and already she was invited to a cool, fancy party at the top of a penthouse suite, no less!

"Cool, I'll be there." Maya rummaged through her wardrobe and found a beautiful black and elegant cocktail dress. As she slipped into her evening dress, Maya wondered what the ratio of men to women was going to be. What were the odds of actually meeting a nice, successful guy who would sweep her off her feet and turn out to be the man of her dreams? *Not that likely*, thought Maya with a sigh. She looked at herself in the mirror. The dress was sleeveless and had a plunging V neck but stopped short of showing off her cleavage. Maya's waistline was petite and so the dress, although figure hugging, was a classy choice. She finished the adornment by wearing long, gold dangling earrings and a simple gold chain. On her feet, she slipped on pointy, three-inch-high stripy black sandals, which she had purchased on a holiday sale from Bloomingdales.

Maya met Toni exactly at 9:30 pm in front of the Manhattan penthouse apartment, and gave her friend a big hug when she saw her. It was great to hang out with Toni; she was such a good friend. Toni's own parents were divorced, so they had a lot in common and had bonded with each other instantly. They had only known each other for a few months in Toronto, as Toni had needed a short-term residence and so had stayed with Maya for a summer term. They had clicked instantly as friends. Toni was a cool girl and had a sarcastic sense of humor, but she was also very intelligent, being a hotshot corporate lawyer. She could debate any matter and was often on the edge of being "in your face" as her opinions were very strong and she had no problem voicing them and pointing out when she thought you were full of "crap." She was a no-nonsense practical girl who did not take any flack from anyone. But she also had a heart of gold underneath and was very protective of her friends. Maya would never forget the time when Toni had confided in her about a "so-called" friend who intended to betray Maya by trying to "steal" her boyfriend at the time. Maya had been hurt and was grateful that Toni had opened her eyes to this person who was clearly not the friend that she had assumed. Toni was fun to be with, but Maya especially loved the fact that she had been so loyal to her.

Toni had brought another girl with her to the party,

a friend of hers from college days from Toronto who had also just moved to Manhattan. When Maya met Sumi (short for Sumitra Chatterjee), she liked her instantly. Both of Sumi's parents were Indian, and she had the beautiful big eyes and the same dark skin tone of Maya's step mom, Sheela. She was very svelte and strikingly beautiful. She was also in her early thirties and Maya instantly felt that this was going to be the beginning of a great friendship between the three of them. Together, Maya, Sumi and Toni entered the grand ballroom of the Manhattan penthouse and were immediately awed by the scene. A huge ornate chandelier lit the room, surrounded by floor-to-ceiling windows, with a breathtaking view of the New York Harbor and the infamous Lady Liberty at the core. The crowds were mostly gathered at the bar and the girls joined the lineup for drinks. They circulated for hours with both friends and acquaintances, and after some time, the girls lost sight of each other in the crowds, and Maya found her alone at the bar.

"Can I buy you a drink?" The voice was deep and masculine, and Maya looked up into the stark blue eyes of a very light-skinned, muscular, tall gentleman. He looked like a football player and Maya instantly felt an attraction to this blond giant. His name was Jason Childs and he worked as a management consultant in midtown Manhattan. They started chatting and she learned that all of his suits were custom made in London, and also that he was a workaholic.

"When I work on a deal, I can go literally for forty-eight hours straight, and sometimes, if I'm lucky, I'll come home to shower the next evening," Jason said with a twinkle in his blue eyes.

"But, of course, I know how to party hard, too. I'm not all work and no play," he continued, chuckling.

Jason told her that he usually stayed at the W Hotel in midtown Manhattan when on assignment for his New York client; however, he had been born and bred in Newport Beach, California. Maya was fascinated by Jason and his stories; they talked for what seemed like endless hours at the bar. Time flew by and eventually, Toni and Sumi found their way to Maya, as the party was coming to and end. Introductions to Maya's new friend were made, and Jason, shortly thereafter, said his goodbyes and left, but not without ensuring he had all of Maya's contact information.

"I think he is really cute," Toni gushed.

Sumi chimed in, "If he has some serious dough and he grew up in Newport Beach, go for it, girl. We all need to marry rich men. Don't you want the option to not work? I know I do."

Maya rolled her eyes. "I don't care how rich he is. At least he won't break my heart like my ex-boyfriend who was Indian and dumped me for family honor."

Toni nodded. She recalled Maya's pain vividly when Amir, Maya's boyfriend of a year, back in Toronto had gone to attend a family wedding in Mumbai and after two weeks, he had arrived back with a fiancée. Apparently, he was introduced to a woman of his own caste in India by his father and had agreed to marry her only after a few meetings. Maya would never forget the way Amir knelt on his knees and begged her forgiveness with tears in his eyes.

"We don't share passion, like you and I, Maya, but she fits well into the family," he had said to her.

With Amir, it had been a choice of respect for his family's wishes; they were Gujarati and his parents had wanted a Gujarati wife. Amir worked in his father's stationary business; he was being groomed to take over and it was a matter of honor and practicality that he wed according to his parent's desires. The heartache left behind by his decision was unfathomable to Amir, as he would never know that Maya was unable to even feel that way about another man for years to come. The emptiness and longing Maya felt after the breakup was the catalyst that had made the decision to move to Manhattan an easy one.

"I'm excited for you, Maya," Sumi gushed on about Jason and how he had looked so handsome in the dark suit he had worn. "I think he's a doll and has a very cute smile."

"Okay, put the breaks on it, Sumi. We have to be cautious; Maya doesn't know him from a hole in the wall, so let's see what happens," Toni said firmly. She didn't trust guys. They said they were going to call, but half the time they were talking through the other half of their mouths.

"I agree," Maya said softly. She liked him but Toni was right. "Let's see what happens."

CHAPTER 3

It was two weeks since the night of the Manhattan penthouse charity event and Maya still had not heard from Jason. It was a Sunday afternoon and Maya's cell phone went off with an indistinguishable number. It was area code 202, Maya felt a flutter in heart when she heard his deep husky voice.

"Hello, Maya, this is Jason. How have you been?"

"I'm good. It's nice to hear from you." Maya responded with a smile in her voice. He had finally called. She was really glad to hear from him.

"I was wondering if you would like to have dinner with me this coming Tuesday," Jason asked.

Maya was thrilled. There was something about Jason that impressed her. She had never met anyone like him before. He was handsome, smart and clearly very successful. He was a partner in his own consulting firm and she thought that he must be brilliant. She couldn't wait to see him. The men in Toronto she had met didn't compare to Jason's level of sophistication. And now he was going to be in town on Tuesday night and wanted to take her to dinner. And at Paper Moon, a high-end Italian restaurant in midtown. Maya was excited and thrilled to be going out with Jason.

The date was everything Maya had dreamed. Jason looked superb in his London-tailored business suit, and easily impressed Maya with his stories of his meetings with chief executive officers and CFO's of public companies. She learned that his clients used Jason to unburden their insecurities about their employees, who they feared would take over their jobs and outshine them one day. And they relied on him to strategize on new markets for new product lines. His work fascinated Maya, as she had never met anyone quite in his league before. He was an ivy-league educated rich boy, born to a multi-millionaire couple who were originally from Texas, but were now settled in Newport Beach, California. His parents traveled the world in their retirement years thus he was alone for the most part and spent the majority of his days and nights working around the clock. He was at his clients' beck and call, and as he described it, he was virtually a slave to his clients. Jason traveled all week long whenever necessary, for even one-hour meetings between cities. He was an experienced world traveler, and would often fly to Europe on a day's notice if necessary. No flight was too long for an important meeting. Maya was taken by Jason and his stories. He made for an incredibly attentive and engaging date. To Maya's delight, the evening ended with a passionate kiss and a promise of more to come.

The romance blossomed and over the next several months, Maya and Jason met for romantic dinners, which occurred for the most part at least once or twice a week. Jason was in town on business during those evenings, and every meeting was wonderful and soon the passion between them became an addiction that Maya could not resist. Maya spent the weekends with her friends, while Jason ended up leaving to go back home to Newport on the weekends. He always claimed that he had to go back on weekends to attend to all the necessary chores of life such as paying bills that had piled up while he was away during the week. And also, he had grown up in California so he welcomed going to his house, which was cozy for him and the place that he could truly call home on the weekends. Maya would have liked to have seen him on the weekends as well, but she was very patient, as it was a burgeoning romance in its infancy. However, as the months flew by, Toni and Sumi started telling her that her patience was overdone.

"So, you still haven't spent a weekend with him? You've been dating him for over three months?" Toni asked.

"He keeps having major deadlines and I don't want to push him. His life is so hectic and he's focused on his career," Maya responded defensively.

"Can you trust the guy? You haven't even seen where he lives. And you don't even know what company he works for. Do you have his business number or his email?" Toni asked.

"No, he said he is old fashioned and doesn't like

email. And I don't want to intrude in his business," Maya responded softly.

Toni shook her head. Why was Maya so gullible? She truly loved her friend and felt protective of her. She didn't trust Jason as far as she could throw him. Her years in Manhattan had taught her to be wary of smooth-talking men, and the fact that in the past eight months he had broken every single one of his promises to Maya, including standing her up twice, and backing out of taking her to his hometown, Newport Beach, did not endear Jason to her in the slightest. But Maya was ready to excuse him on every occasion. *Didn't her relationship with Amir teach her to be wary of men and not so trusting?* Toni thought. Her heart was protective of Maya, but regardless of how critical Toni was of Jason, it was apparent that her words had little effect on Maya.

Toni just doesn't get it, Maya thought, as she dressed for her next dinner date with Jason. She had told both Toni and Sumi about Jason's big secret. They knew that Jason had had a fiancée who had died in a car crash only three years ago. Jason had lived with his former fiancée for over seven years and they had planned their life together to the tee. Apparently, they had met in college and he had known her for over ten years. Jason needed to take it slow in his next relationship, and Maya understood this; she was a patient woman and her heart went out for the intense pain that Jason must have suffered over the loss of his fiancée. She secretly hoped that their blossoming relationship would pave a new path for them both.

Maya was looking forward to spending the next evening with Jason. He was taking her to a new trendy

Sushi restaurant in midtown. She was also hopeful that he would suggest taking her back with him on the weekend, so that she could see his home in Newport and the area where he had lived for so long. She knew that Toni was right; more than enough time had passed for her to request seeing his hometown. The evening flew by, as it normally did with Jason. After three hours of conversation and drinks at the fancy Sushi restaurant in midtown, Maya found herself passionately locked in Jason's embrace at his regular penthouse suite on the top floor of the W Hotel.

"I missed you," whispered Jason in Maya's ears after their passion had subsided and the aftermath of their lovemaking left them exhausted in each other's arms.

"I did too," Maya responded softly, gazing into the blue eyes that left her melting inside.

"Are we going to finally do a vacation together or spend a weekend? It seems like every time we make plans, something comes up or gets in the way," Maya said, looking at him wistfully.

"I know, I feel bad, but this is the nature of the beast. Consulting is a very demanding job. Be patient, sweetie. We are definitely going to go away together. I want to spend time with you as well. We'll make it work. I'll call you next week with the dates I can get away," Jason responded.

"Okay. I hope it's soon, but I'll wait." *Do I have a choice?*, Maya thought in her head. *Maybe my friends are right and I deserve a lot more.* But she was fascinated by Jason's connections, his status and his lifestyle. And the best part of their relationship was that when they were together, Maya felt like she was the only woman in his world. There was a way that Jason had that made her feel special. When they were together, he listened to her raptly and never forgot a word she said to him. This was a rare quality in a man; *most of them*, she thought, *couldn't remember half of what a woman told them*. But, he always listened to her intently and knew how to say the right thing at the right time.

When the alarm buzzed loudly in the morning, Maya woke up and after a quick shower, she gave Jason a quick kiss goodbye, as he was still lying in bed. She waited in front of the elevators and noticed a Hispanic maid, pushing her cart, who was coming towards her. The maid looked at her with a shy smile and Maya smiled back and said sweetly to her, "Would you have anymore of those Bliss hand lotions?" She loved the smell of Bergamot and Sage, and hoped the maid had extra travel sizes.

The maid responded, "Of course. You are staying with Mr. Casey in Room 4501? I just noticed you came from his room."

Maya shook her head "Room 4501?" She repeated. Maya had just come from that suite, but, of course, Jason's last name was Childs.

"Of course, that is Mr. Casey's regular penthouse suite, but you already knew that," the maid smiled. "I have seen you with him a few times."

"Yes, yes, that is right." Maya's head was spinning. Who was Mr. Casey? She was dating Jason Childs and he was the regular customer that stayed in 4501, wasn't he? Or maybe there was another gentleman that stayed there whom the maid was confusing him with? Surely, she had made a mistake.

Hurriedly, Maya left the hotel building and her heart was pounding the entire time she was on the subway train. Once she arrived at her office cubicle at work, she dialed the front desk of the W Hotel. The clerk answered "Hello, W Hotel, how may I help you?"

"Could you connect me to room 4501, I believe a Mr. Childs is staying there."

The hotel clerk responded "There is no one by that name."

"I apologize, I meant a Mr. Casey." Maya's head was whirling. What was Jason's last name, Casey or Childs?

"John Casey has already checked out, ma'am."

Maya stared at the phone in shock. Who on earth was Jason Childs then? It looked like she had just been led on by a complete double-crossing, smooth-talking consultant who had not even given her his legitimate name! Her mind raced. Was Jason married and if so, was that the reason he had never taken her to his hometown? She shook her head — if home was even Newport Beach, that is. Maya was in an entire state of confusion. He was Jason Childs, not John Casey, or was it truly the other way around?

Over the next couple of weeks, she waited to hear from Jason. In her mind, Maya had replayed all of the long conversations she had had with him over the past few months. There had to be a mistake. The next few weeks were agonizing until finally on a Tuesday morning she received a text from Jason. "I want to see you tonight. Also, Bahamas, let's go next month? Let's

over again how she could have been so taken in by this seemingly polished and charming man.

In the morning, she received a text from Jason, "Where are you? Why did you leave?" Maya ignored the text, but if she thought that was the end of Jason, she was mistaken. It was like a fire lit up underneath Jason. For the next month, she was constantly hounded by phone and text messages from him. But Maya was angry and she felt foolish that she had been played by a smooth and suave businessman who wasn't even who he said he was. She had acknowledged the truth to herself, that he had deceived her, and that he was likely married and was using her for a good time in the city. She was so humiliated and embarrassed that she kept the entire incident to herself for a good month.

When Maya stopped hearing from Jason, she was ready to tell Toni and Sumi what had happened. Embarrassment had kept her quiet on her discovery, but these were her best friends and they had a right to know. The three of them were meeting for dinner at the Fives restaurant at Hotel Peninsula on Fifth Avenue.

Maya had tears in her eyes when she told her story.

"Asshole, I knew he was a creep from the ghetto," said Toni. She was very upset and although she wanted to say 'I told you so,' she held her tongue, as Maya was already upset enough.

"This is totally surreal. At least you had some good sex for eight months," said Sumi, rolling her eyes. " Both girls looked at her. Sumi was a classic A-type personality and worked as a sales trader at a premier investment bank on Wall Street. Her boyfriend of four years lived in Toronto, but was moving next month to Manhattan to be close to Sumi. He had proposed many times, but Sumi kept putting him off. She was a very practical girl with a no-nonsense attitude, and she was in absolutely no rush to settle down. Furthermore, she would not be pressured into marrying her boyfriend until she was good and ready, and right now she was having way too much fun.

"I feel like a moron. I've been dating someone who doesn't exist. He didn't even give me his real name. He probably has a wife and three kids," Maya said.

"Girls, from here on in we get business cards, we Google them and get home, work and cell numbers. We need to be intelligent here; there are tons of filthy, lying con artists out there," Toni said, raising her glass.

The three of them raised and clinked their wine glasses, and toasted to Toni's sentiment. Later that night, Maya's heart ached. Once again, for the second time in her life, she had been completely duped by a boyfriend. How was it possible that this could happen again? Did she have a sign on her forehead, saying, "I am a sucker"? Finally, after tossing and turning several times over the course of the night, her eyelids became heavy and she was lost to the images in her dreams that were vague and scattered, and would be completely indiscernible when dawn arrived.

CHAPTER 4

Maya's first year in Manhattan was over, and the next few years quickly flew by. They were filled by a blur of late-night weekend parties and constant vacationing. Maya had made many friends and acquaintances, and with her friendly and charming manner, it was easy for her to draw people in. Each year, Maya would fly down south to a different Caribbean island with a close friend from Toronto. Usually it was either Ida or Renee that would accompany her. On long weekends, she would often travel with various local friends to larger metropolitan cities, such as Las Vegas, Miami or San Francisco. There was so much to do and see here in the United States. Maya's love of the hot sun and beaches earned her the nickname of "Caribbean Queen" among her friends.

On the weekends, Maya's favorite pastime was to volunteer for Junior Achievement. She enjoyed traveling to the schools for underprivileged children in areas such as Harlem and Brooklyn, where she and a group of volunteers would spend one day a month either painting or decorating a classroom. Maya also volunteered her time to City Meals on Wheels, a not for profit that organized meals for senior citizens and held fundraising events throughout the year. She loved donating her free time for worthy causes and her community service kept her balanced with the rest of her social life.

One of Maya's favorite moments of Manhattan was hosting a joint party with Toni at a local Upper West Side sports club. They had negotiated with the owners of the bar to host a party with a confirmed number of ticket sales in exchange for airing the final episode of "Seinfeld" on their large flat screen TV's. The ticket price included beer and wings along with a seat at the bar. Maya and Toni sold approximately one hundred tickets to friends and acquaintances. Although the season's final episode itself was a bit of a disappointment to the audience, the party was a huge success, as everyone enjoyed beer and wings and cheered the show, which was known to have one of the most amazingly long runs in TV history. Maya had arranged to have a small wholesale company design a black t-shirt that highlighted "Seinfeld, the final episode" in large bold and white letters on its front. Each guest received the t-shirt as a memoir. Maya and Toni were both thrilled that they had pulled off such an enormously successful and fun-filled event. The icing on the cake was making a small profit from the ticket sales. Toni had sold a larger number of tickets sales as she knew many more people than Maya, having lived in Manhattan for several years longer. However, Maya didn't mind. She had sold her fair share of the tickets and was ecstatic that she was the co-hostess of a "last episode Seinfeld party" at a cool sports bar on the Upper West Side.

Life was good and Maya had made up her mind to have a good time as a single girl in the city. She dated with pure fun and no serious intention. None of the men she dated struck a romantic chord with her. She didn't have the heart to take anyone too seriously after her experience with Jason. She casually dated a gentleman who insisted on wearing cowboy boots on his dates with her, and he admitted to being a professional line dancer on Friday nights. She once asked him jokingly, albeit with a hint of seriousness, "What do you wear to the beach?" He chose to ignore the question and Maya knew very quickly that this wasn't a match made in heaven.

She also went out a couple of times with a very attractive gentleman who was a high school teacher that kept two dogs and a cat in his house. He was a very artsy individual and their lack of common interests quickly extinguished the initial attraction. A series of men came into Maya's life who briefly kept her amused and entertained, but no one person came close to piercing the shield that she had built as a result of her past relationships. However, there had been one handsome gentleman whom she had met through Toni at a neighborhood bar. John was a business associate of Toni's but worked at a different law firm. They had hit it off and she and John had enjoyed a few dates together, but Maya soon became suspicious of him, as he had not offered to give her his home number. Her experience with Jason had taught her to be wary. She told her office assistant Linda about him, who always enjoyed hearing about Maya's dating experiences. Linda was a very fashionable woman in her early fifties, who was happily married and had raised two daughters. She loved to gossip with Maya about office affairs and hear about Maya's love life. She sympathized with Maya and agreed with her about how difficult it was to find a good man in the city.

It was bothering Maya that John had not given her his home number after their two dates, and so towards the end of the business day she walked over to Linda's desk to discuss this issue.

"Linda, do you not think it is strange that John only calls me from work and he has never given me his home number? I like him, but I hope he is not another Jason. I only have his work number."

Linda looked up at Maya, shaking her head. She was a brunette with auburn highlights in her hair, which she liked to style differently every month. Her hands were perfectly manicured with a bright red polish.

"Yes, I do think that is strange. Be careful. These men in New York are such players and they don't seem to want to commit. My nephew is the same way. He's dating such a nice girl, she's very attractive and his parents love her, but it's been two years and he still doesn't want to get married." Linda sighed. It was exasperating for her sister and brother-in-law, as they both wanted their thirty-five-year-old son married off and couldn't for the life of them understand why he hadn't proposed.

"So what do you think I should do?" Maya asked. She respected Linda's opinions immensely and relied on Linda to give her solid advice.

"Well, why don't you try to find out his house number and call? Just to be sure he doesn't have a wife," responded Linda.

Maya went back to her desk and looked up John's home number in Hoboken, New Jersey. The phone rang a few times and a woman's voice answered.

"Hello."

"Hi, I was wondering if John is home. I'm an old friend of his from Calgary." Maya recalled that John had told her he had once lived in Calgary. She hoped she sounded believable.

"He's at work right now, but I can pass on the message," the unidentified voice said.

"Yes, please tell him its Kathy calling. And who is this?" Maya asked.

"This is his fiancée. You can call him back after seven. He should be home by then."

"Thanks." Maya hung up the phone and rushed to Linda's desk with a scowl and related her discovery.

"I can't believe the gall of that man. He is getting married and yet he is asking you out. Nothing about men surprises me anymore. I'm glad you didn't waste time with him, Maya. You have so much to give and I know you will find the right person," Linda assured her with confidence.

And that was the end of John. Maya was glad she had checked on him and she quickly put it behind her. She needed a serious break from men and didn't have the heart or inclination to focus on a serious relationship.

Maya really enjoyed working with her colleagues at the office. Linda was her confidante and her boss;

Charlie was so protective of her. A client had once called Maya to ask her out for dinner and drinks, and she had confessed to Charlie that she was unsure if she should go. Immediately, Charlie responded in his thick Bronx accent.

"That's up to you. But if he tries anything, I will personally slug him."

Maya laughed and told Linda later that day what Charlie had said. Linda looked at her.

"Well, did you know that Charlie had a daughter who would have been about your age had she lived?"

"What do you mean? What happened to her?" Maya's heart sank.

"She died in a car accident when she was only fifteen. Charlie is divorced and we're all pretty sure that's the reason. He doesn't want to get married again. That's why he's been living with a woman for the past ten years. But he won't marry her."

Maya felt a lump in her throat form for Charlie. She had no idea about the hardship that he had undergone in his life. He was such a kind, fatherly soul and so intelligent. He was much respected amongst the senior management team and was also known to be extremely supportive of his own staff. She felt lucky that he was her boss and so sad for him that he had undergone this terrible misfortune. It was even more tragic that his marriage had not survived the tragedy of losing their only child.

Maya went back to her desk and finished booking her flight for the upcoming weekend. It was mid-April and she, Toni and Sumi were celebrating Toni's birthday in Puerto Rico. The resort, known as El Conquistador, was breathtaking and it looked like a long, white castle set upon a steep hill. The resort's cable car took the guests down towards the white sandy beachfront and turquoise-colored ocean. The yellow villas at the foot of the cable car were where the girls were staying and when they arrived at their room, all three were so excited to head towards the beach that they hurriedly donned their clothes to put on their bathing suits.

After a long swim in the Atlantic, Toni and Maya went to shower in their hotel room. It was the first night from a long, hot day in the sun and both were exhausted. Sumi had picked up a hot, young German blond who had been immediately taken by her dark beauty and they were both enjoying a date on their first night at the resort's finest Italian restaurant. Sumi was a forward and voluptuous female who often went from man to man without worrying about what anyone thought. Her philosophy on life was very simple: until you were actually married, you were allowed to have as much fun as you can. The fact that she had a long-time boyfriend did not stop her in the least. Surin had asked her on many occasion to marry him; however, Sumi kept pushing him off, and her friends often wondered why she just didn't cut him loose. It didn't seem fair to him, but the girls also viewed him as a bit of a lap dog, since he had what seemed like never ending patience with Sumi.

Maya came out of the shower draped in a white towel and started combing her hair in front of the dresser while Toni watched, sprawled on the bed. "Oops," Maya's towel went tumbling down and her naked body glistened with the last remnants of the drops of water. Toni's eyes widened and she felt slivers of perspiration form on her own skin. Maya had a perfect figure, with breasts that stood upright, virtually a flat abdomen and a slight curvature of hips that were neither too wide nor narrow. Toni recalled her time as a freshman when she had roomed with a Puerto Rican girl in her college dorm and they had made out together passionately and explored each other's bodies for hours that night. Toni had been embarrassed the next morning, and the shame of what she had done had stopped Toni from ever repeating the incident for several years to come. Her roommate had kept quiet as well, since she herself was bisexual, but didn't wish to embarrass Toni, knowing that Toni was a virgin who had not come out of the closet.

After her rendezvous with her roommate, Toni had dated men and explored a relationship with a young British man named Robbie in Manhattan, which had lasted a year. But Toni's heart had never been into it; she simply didn't feel the same draw that she did to females. Ever since Maya and Sumi had moved to the city, the secret had stayed buried in Toni, as she was afraid of being judged by her new best friends. Toni had not yet found a partner, but she had had many sexual and brief relationships with other women in Manhattan that she had kept from the girls. Maya and Sumi had simply thought that she hadn't yet met the right man, so the truth had stayed buried within Toni ever since she had know them.

"Sorry about that," Maya was shy to be caught naked, even in front of her girlfriend. She quickly pulled a rose-colored, sleeveless, flower-printed dress and donned it over her.

Toni was looking at her in a slightly strange manner. "I'm not sure how to tell you this." Tears rolled down her cheeks.

"What's wrong?" Maya said.

"I think I might be...well, I haven't found a man that really turns me on. Maya, I prefer to be with a woman. And I mean sexually."

"What?" It took a few seconds for Maya to absorb the impact of what Toni was admitting. "Do you mean, you're...well you might be gay?" Maya was shocked inside; she had no indication of her friend's inclinations at all.

Toni wiped the tears from her cheeks and her voice was clearer. "Maya, I am gay." I have been a lesbian for the last seven years, and probably before that...I didn't know how to tell you; I guess I was a bit nervous of what you and Sumi would think." The relief to actually let it out and reveal her secret was overwhelming for Toni. It had been too difficult to keep it from her best friend. Toni had started having certain sexual feelings for Maya, which had been ignited this evening when she had seen her friend's naked body.

"Why didn't you tell me this before? You shouldn't have kept this from us." Maya gave Toni a hug. "Sumi will understand as well. We can't help feeling what we feel or who we are. It doesn't change who you are as a person. I still love you the same." She asked the next question hesitantly, "Is there someone that you are interested in?"

"No, there is no one right now." How could Toni

reveal her feelings for Maya when she knew that her friend was looking for the man of her dreams and not for a woman?

"Well, you better tell me when there is," Maya said coolly. She respected Toni's choices, however, she was a bit dumbfounded that Toni had kept this secret for so long.

The next morning, Toni told Sumi the truth as well, and although Sumi's reaction was a bit less charitable than Maya's, she supported her friend as well. Being a bit of a nymphomaniac, Sumi couldn't really relate to Toni, but she also had respect for her friend's choices and didn't pass judgment on her. The last night in Puerto Rico, the three friends ended up celebrating Toni's thirty-fifth birthday with a big bang. Hip hop and rock music filled the air at the resort's nightclub where the three partied till four in the morning, and where Toni felt free to hit on women openly, and Sumi and Maya flirted with the all the available single, hot men.

CHAPTER 5

It was a sunny Saturday afternoon in August and Maya was taking a stroll through Central Park, and it seemed as if all of Manhattan's residents were strolling, biking or blading. She passed the famous Imagine circle in Strawberry Fields, where tourists still gathered around, holding bouquets in their hands to pay tribute to the late John Lennon. The smell of the water lilies filled the air with a fresh aroma and Maya enjoyed her walk when her cell phone rang.

"Hi Sheila, how are you?" It was her step mom and after the initial pleasantries and inquiries about Maya's love life, Sheela got right to the point.

"Maya, I have a man for you. And I think he is perfect for you; he lives in Ohio and he has nice mid-western values. He is very handsome, and I know his aunt very well; she is from Newfoundland. And she says he is ready to settle down, so I think you should meet him."

"What does he do?" Maya wasn't crazy about neither the Ohio deal nor about being fixed up, but she felt as if she had to humor Sheela.

"His parents are from New Jersey, and he will be going there in a few weeks. Ashok is a doctor and has a very successful practice. Can I give him your number, Maya?"

Maya laughed, "No way." If Sheila thought she was going to fix her up with some Indian doctor, she could forget it. Although she knew her step mom's heart was in the right place, there was no way she was going to meet some random Indian guy that was her parent's friend's son. He was probably a geek with horn-rimmed glasses and Maya had no intention of wasting her time.

"Okay, talk to your dad then," Sheila gave the phone to Maya's dad.

In his soft voice, Maya's father stated his case pleadingly.

"Maya, please we are really worried about you; we want the best for you and what do you have to lose by just meeting Ashok? If you don't like him, that's fine, we won't pressure you...but, please we need you to be serious about your life now. You are way too picky and I want to see you settle down now," he said. Raj didn't mention her age, but it concerned him that his daughter was thirty-seven years old and was still not married.

Maya sighed. She had a soft spot for her father. It was all the unconditional love that he had given her all these years. Also, she was very aware of the rough time her mother had given him when he had lost his job. The fact that her mother had run off to Italy and had an affair just before the divorce had made it ten times worse for her father.

"Okay, fine, you can give him my number," she relented. What choice did she have? She would do her duty and meet him to please her parents. Maybe she would like him, thought Maya ruefully. But probably not, she confessed to herself.

Three weeks went by and Maya finally heard from Ashok. They initially chatted briefly on the phone, and the conversation was pleasant enough. He mentioned that he would come to town at the end of the month to visit his parents who lived in Somerset, New Jersey. They set up a meeting for the weekend that he would be arriving, and to Maya, this was truly a blind date, since she really had no idea what he looked like or what to expect.

Maya woke up on a Saturday afternoon in mid-September, the day that she was finally going to meet Ashok after having conversed with him on the phone a few times over the past several weeks. As their first date was taking place during the day, Maya decided to dress casually in a comfortable pair of jeans and a fitted black V-neck sweater. There was no reason to don her finest wardrobe when she didn't even know what he looked like. She briskly walked up Amsterdam Avenue to meet Ashok at SaraBeth's, which was located on the Upper West Side, very close to her apartment. When she arrived, she was surprised to see a good-looking Indian man, almost six feet tall with beautiful dark eyes and long lashes, as well as a small, neatly trimmed moustache above his full lips. He was waiting outside the restaurant.

Sarabeth was a famous brunch place on the Upper West Side and was highly coveted for its dining, as was evidenced by the crowd waiting outside in usual New York fashion. Ashok shook her hand and told her that the wait time for a table was well over half an hour. This was typical in Manhattan; people flocked to the best-known restaurants, creating lineups and crowds that easily waited an hour to dine. During the time they waited for a table, Maya was pleasantly surprised to learn that she had much in common with Ashok. Toronto was one of his favorite cities and he related that he had cousins that lived there whom he visited on a regular basis. Ashok was also born in Montreal, which made him a Canadian, like Maya. They had much in common and over a hearty brunch, she also learned he was an avid Yankees fan, and also loved tennis, which was Maya's favorite sport. The conversation turned to politics and Ashok expressed his views in no uncertain terms.

"Bush is an idiot. He lied to the American people. There were no weapons of mass destruction. Saddam Hussein may be an evil man, but to send our troops to Iraq without proof is the worst thing he has done for our country." Ashok was vehement in his response, but it wasn't the case that he was an extreme leftist; rather, he simply disagreed with the decisions that the current president had made. He believed that the focus after 9/11 should have been to continue to find Bin Laden and break the terrorist's networks and cells, which he believed to be the cause of the events leading to the largest civilian attack in US history. He was also of the opinion that the current president had damaged many important relationships with foreign countries, and that the perceptions and image of the US to the foreign world would be adversely affected for a long time.

"I know, I feel so bad for our troops and I totally get why we needed to go into Afghanistan; Bin Laden is still hiding out there, but why Iraq? This war seems so unnecessary," Maya sighed.

In his deep voice, Ashok responded. "Because it was personal. Bush wanted revenge against Saddam for attempting to assassinate his father, George H. W. Bush in the 1991 Gulf War."

"I agree," Maya said. She was in sync with Ashok about US foreign policies and agreed that the current President, George W. Bush, and his administration were completely fixated on the wrong ideas about the war, and as a consequence, had made the wrong choices. They both conversed for a couple more hours on politics, family and career. Time flew by and it was clear that there was a mutual interest and connection.

Before Ashok left to take the train back to New Jersey, he kissed Maya on the cheek and promised to call her soon. Maya went back to her apartment with a warm feeling in her heart; she liked him and wanted to see him again soon. There was definitely potential there!

The phone rang and it was Sheila. "Honey, what do you think?"

This was the major problem with being set up; it became everyone's business and then the matchmakers would also require updates as well. Maya responded sweetly, rolling her eyes at the same time, "I do like him and we'll see each other again. But, Sheela, no interference or pressure, please! I just want to get to know him on my own."

Sheela promised she wouldn't play cupid anymore now that she knew Maya liked Ashok. She only wanted to get a sense of whether she had done right by Maya. She crossed her fingers and hoped that Maya and Ashok would find love and eventually marry. She knew all of the heartaches that her stepdaughter had gone through and she didn't think that anyone deserved to have gone through that much hurt. She loved Maya like her own daughter and thought of her as a beautiful woman who deserved to have a good man and a family of her own. She was concerned that Maya was thirty-seven years old and that her biological clock was getting to be on the wrong side of procreating.

Ashok courted Maya over the next several months, and the distance between them was hard but made easier by the long phone conversations they would have at night. Initially, they spoke every other day, but the intensity became so great that they soon needed to talk at least a few times a day. Ashok had a very busy schedule, as he ran his own medical practice with another physician. Being a gentleman, he flew Maya out to his hometown in Ohio on alternate weekends for the first few months of their courtship. Each weekend that Maya spent with him was romantic and adventurous. Maya felt at home in Ashok's large house; it was cozy and tastefully furnished and they would often cuddle in front of the fireplace in his large living room, which was lit by real wood that Ashok had cut down from the trees in his backyard. He was a real handyman and he had built his deck, with the help of two close friends, in the span of one day. He had also finished his basement including all of the fancy electrical wiring by himself. He would often joke with Maya that he had the best tools "in the shop" and it was no wonder she had fallen for him. And Maya did fall in love with him, as she was swept away by the passion between them and the fun, easy conversations they shared. She also loved his witty and dry sense of humor. It was obvious that Ashok's family and friends meant the world to him. Maya also fell in love with his family. He had taken her to meet them at their home in New Jersey only after four months of dating. His parents treated her with much affection and it was obvious that they liked her right away. His mother was a traditional woman and initially was somewhat cautious with Maya, as she observed her and watched more during the first meeting rather than opening up right away. However, Ashok's father embraced her warmly, as if she was already the new daughter-in-law to be. His sister and brother-in-law were also there at dinner, and they seemed to have an easygoing rapport with each other. It was clear to Maya that theirs was a very close family. She had fun with them and was happy that her boyfriend's family was warm and easy to be with.

It was New Year's Eve and Ashok had flown down to spend the weekend with Maya in Manhattan. They had decided to have a romantic weekend and stay overnight at the Le Park Meridian on 57th Street and Park Avenue. Ashok had booked dinner on New Year's Eve in Tribecca at the restaurant Bouley, the trendy French bistro owned by the famous chef, David Bouley. After a lovely dinner and toast to the new year, they hailed a taxi-cab back to the hotel where Maya and Ashok made love tenderly and passionately throughout the night, which was the perfect entrée into New Year's Day. After a satisfying brunch at the hotel, they spent the rest of the day enjoying a long walk through Central Park, which was full of snow-capped trees and lovers strolling hand in hand. One of Ashok's favorite movies was "Gone with the Wind" and coincidentally, it was playing on television when they arrived at Maya's apartment. That evening they cuddled on the couch, watching Clark Gable and Vivien Leigh in the aftermath of the Civil war. The weekend flew by too quickly and when Ashok left to go back to Ohio the next day, Maya was literally in tears.

Ashok's best friends were a married couple, Smyla and Roddy, whom he had known for over a decade. The four of them would meet for dinners together whenever Maya was in Ohio. It seemed as if she had known them forever. Smyla was much like Ashok; she was quieter and more serious with a dry wit, and Maya was more like Roddy; they were both gregarious and outgoing and liked to chat at high speed. The foursome became very close and shared many laughs over drinks. The girls would enjoy apple martinis while the boys indulged in fine scotch. Maya loved to cook and often she would host pizza parties for the four of them at Ashok's place. Life was indeed perfect and it was Maya's greatest wish that she and Ashok would start a life together soon as a married couple and begin the process of raising a family.

It was May 2005 and Ashok and Maya had dated

for over eight months. Ashok had met Toni and Sumi several times over the course of his visits with Maya in Manhattan. They both liked Ashok immensely, as he easily charmed them with his dry wit and intelligent conversation. He also teased Maya immensely in front of them and they believed that he loved her with all of his heart. Both were also very curious as to when he would pop the question to her. Ashok's mother had also grown to love Maya, and she would often call her and tell Maya stories about Ashok from the days he was a young boy, learning about cars and engines from his father. Maya loved listening to her stories, which made her feel as if she was part of the family. Maya started to get caught up in the fantasy of what her life would be like with Ashok. Although Ohio wasn't her first choice to live, she felt she was ready for the suburban lifestyle that married live with Ashok would offer. And her heart was into him, although she was very aware of the fact that a life in Ohio would be a stark contrast to the hectic pace of Manhattan.

CHAPTER 6

"I am not getting married," Ashok said matter-of-factly in no uncertain terms. Maya was at his house in Ohio where they were having a tense conversation about where their relationship was going.

"What?" Maya was taken aback. She knew Ashok was stubborn. He had shown signs of being a difficult person at times, but since Maya was so easygoing and brushed off moodiness, she had not been bothered by it. Roddy had often joked about Ashok's personality and how he would require a woman with saint-like qualities to put up with him. He once said that he had traveled for two days with Ashok on a long drive and there were so many rules that Ashok had in his car that Roddy had decided he would rather fly alone next time rather than succumb to all of Ashok's rules. The ribbing was in jest though and Maya had never taken the bantering seriously.

"Are you afraid of marriage?" Maya asked.

"Yes, I think I am commitment phobic. Too many bad marriages out there, honey. Why can't we just date for two years and see what happens?"

"Because I am thirty-eight years old, that's why; we shouldn't need two years and if you want to have a family, then isn't it going to be that much harder to have kids? These are all things we should think about if you want to have a family." Maya was frustrated. She thought they been clear about the direction of the relationship. They had many conversations earlier in their relationship regarding their desires to raise a family.

"But that shouldn't be the reason to get married, just to have kids. Lots of bad marriages out there and I don't want to be one of them," Ashok said firmly.

Maya fought her rising temper. She chose to let it go. What was she fighting against? It was clear that he wasn't budging. The one quality she had come to know about Ashok was his stubbornness. When he made up his mind about something, she knew that it would be like moving mountains to try to change it.

The rest of the weekend went relatively smoothly, although Ashok had given Maya a lot to think about. She knew that he had had some bad experiences in a previous relationship. Ashok had been in an on-and-off relationship for over eight years with a woman whom he had loved, but who had constantly disappointed him in terms of commitment. She had eventually cheated on him and Ashok had discovered her infidelity by accident one day. He had been searching for homes in the area on his computer, and discovered that she had purchased a house with another man. The discovery had pained him, as it was confirmation that she had been a two timer and that she had taken him for a ride for many long years. But there was a point, when Ashok had taken her back a few times over the course of those years and although this was unfathomable to Maya, she was quite sure that his volatile relationship had affected him deeply. It was no wonder he had such deep rooted fears and was gunshy about making a commitment. His mother had hated Ashok's girlfriend and confided in Maya that she truly believed that "the woman had done a number on him, and she's the reason my son is still single at thirty-nine." He was simply "screwed over" by one woman who had had a catastrophic effect on him.

Back home in Manhattan, it was a Saturday afternoon and the three girlfriends were in line for a book signing event at Barnes and Nobles on the Upper East Side. A famous author, who was deemed a relationship expert, was hosting a book-signing event for her new book titled *Men and Commitment*. Toni, Sumi and Maya attended the event together after enjoying their regular weekend brunch. The speaker had told the audience (who were a large group of single girls in their thirties and forties interested in hooking men and then keeping them committed for life) that they were welcome to ask the author one question while she was signing an autograph for the book. Sumi and Toni were amused and really didn't have much interest in acquiring the book, but were both humored by the event and waited patiently for Maya, who was in line.

When Maya's turn came, she posed the question to

the author, "Do you think it is reasonable for a man to commit to a woman after eight months of dating?

The author looked at her and very bluntly responded, "If he can't commit after eight months, get rid of him and move on."

Toni nodded her head and said to Maya, "I guess she knows what she is talking about, being a relationship expert and all."

But Sumi disagreed, "I don't think so; if she is such an expert why is she still single?" But the words had already made a mark on Maya. What should she do about Ashok? She did want to have kids and raise a family. Was it fair for him to ask her to date for two years and for her to take the risk that he would commit after that time? And what if he never did? Would she be wasting time with someone who would never be able to figure things out? She knew that in the Indian culture, relationships developed quickly and decisions about marriage were made on a much shorter timeframe than western-type relationships. Although Maya was half-Indian, she was not bound by the arranged-marriage traditions of so many stricter East Indian families. She had been brought up in a very western culture; her parents had been divorced since she was ten years old and it had taken her a long time to believe in the institution of marriage. But now she was ready and wanted to live life with a good, decent man and raise a family.

Ashok was fully East Indian and had been raised with strong family values, but when it came to relationships, he had similar views to most Americans. Most of his friends were White, football-loving males that were interested in long relationships but not necessarily marriage. Maya was confused. Men were men; it didn't matter what culture they came from if they were raised here, in America. She wasn't sure if Ashok would ever commit; perhaps he would decide he would rather remain a bachelor for life. How deep were his commitment issues? She wished she knew the answers to all these questions. A crystal ball would have come in pretty handy at that moment.

It was a late Friday afternoon and Maya was in her office, pondering over their relationship when she decided then and there that she needed to confront Ashok and have a heart to heart talk with him. She had waited to meet the right man her whole life and she knew Ashok was by no means perfect. He had even shown symptoms of a temper that could flare easily when he was irked. He would be no easy man to live with, as he had weird quirks such as being very fanatical about cleanliness. If there was a single crumb that fell on the counter, he immediately would take a cloth to scrub it furiously. And he was also very set in his ways so that any change in his routine affected his equilibrium and created moodiness in him. But what could Maya do? Despite his moodiness, she did love him and she knew him to be a kind, decent man whose company she enjoyed.

She rang Ashok at five o'clock and as his secretary recognized her voice, she immediately put her through to him.

"Hi there," Maya said in response to Ashok's voice.

"Hey, what's going on?" Ashok was wrapping up his notes from his appointments for the day.

"Just wanted to say hi and see how you're doing," Maya responded softly.

"Looking forward to a relaxing weekend. I have stuff to fix around the house," Ashok said.

"Won't you miss me?" Maya asked.

"Yes, of course, Maya. But there's nothing wrong with having some time apart." Ashok valued his independence and freedom greatly.

"I miss you and want to be with you. More than that, I have been thinking a lot about having children. I really want to have kids, Ashok, and I don't think we should wait that much longer. Don't you think you know me well enough to make a decision?" Maya didn't mince her words. She had waited so long to say them.

"Maya, I love you, and I do know you well enough to make a decision. But I am not sure that I want to be tied down right now. What if it doesn't work out; what if we grow apart, like so many couples do? Why ruin what we have now?" Ashok said a bit impatiently.

"Because I don't want to waste time. We should move on to the next stage of our lives now. We are both old enough, and if you can't take the chance with me, who will you be able to take the chance with?" Maya was equally impatient.

What was wrong with Ashok? He had often commented about being happy to be in such a healthy relationship, and that it was so refreshing not to fight constantly. And most of all, his time with her was peaceful. His mother had told him in no uncertain terms that this was how it should be instead of the crazy roller coaster ride he had had with his ex-girlfriend for years.

"Okay, I guess you have made your decision, now it's my turn to make mine," Ashok responded coolly. He even sounded a bit annoyed.

"Yes, you need you to make yours, I don't want to waste anymore time," Maya said, her voice totally exasperated. They hung up and Maya went home, feeling like this was not really the way it should be; that she had just had a major fight with her best friend. She felt frustrated and sad at the same time. Ashok had been her best friend for the past year.

The next two months were the most agonizing and gut wrenching of Maya's life. She spent hours analyzing Ashok, discussing him and the potential outcome of their relationship with her friends. Surprisingly, one of her main advocates was Ashok's mother. Almost every other day, his mother would call her, discussing Ashok and how highly he spoke of Maya. She was very positive about the outcome between the two, but secretly feared that Ashok was letting his past relationships ruin his chances for the future with a wonderful girl. Maya's step mom, Sheela was also of great comfort to her and told her to be positive, that Ashok would come through for her. She also agreed that it was time for him to make a decision. They were both old enough to know what they wanted and mature to make an intelligent decision. Sheela had waited an entire year for Maya's own father to commit to her, as Natasha had burned him badly. But Sheela had shown Raj that their love could weather the ups and downs they would face, and that she was committed to resolving any issues they would have with open and honest communication. They also shared more in common than he ever had with his Canadian wife; they understood and appreciated their own culture, they both loved Indian food and had similar family values. Above all else, they knew that they would do their best to work through life together. Neither would be as selfish and unyielding as to put their own desires above their marriage.

The weeks went by and when Ashok did call Maya, the conversations were very brief and neutral. Ashok himself couldn't figure out what was preventing him from moving forward and constantly agonized about why he couldn't just propose to Maya. His sister had often accused him of needing a shrink, and lately she had been very vocal in repeating her advice. He had suffered greatly from his breakup with his ex-girlfriend, which had occurred a few years into the relationship. They had broken up when he had discovered she had been two-timing him. Nonetheless, after a year of wooing him and sending him flowers and crying, he had taken her back. This roller coaster of his had been going on for over eight years, and neither Ashok's sister nor mother had been impressed with what they viewed to be self-abusive behaviour. This was the first time Ashok had been free of her for over two years, and they both felt that it was time that a nice girl like Maya had finally come along for him and that he should be thankful. But life wasn't quite that simple and Ashok's heart had been dented and needed a long time to heal. Although he loved Maya, the question of whether he was ready to completely trust again and take a leap of faith was the primary issue.

Finally, Ashok called her to let her know that he was

flying into New York for the weekend and that he would like to see her early Saturday afternoon. He said he was only available for a short while and his tone warned Maya that there would not be any proposal imminent. The night before he called, Maya had slept very restlessly and furthermore, it felt like sleep had evaded her over the past couple of months. The next day, when Ashok showed up at her apartment, her heart was pounding when she opened the door. Ashok stood there awkwardly carrying a large bag, which was full of her clothes and personal belongings that she had left in his house. She felt tears form when she saw the bag and Ashok's face was white as a ghost when he looked up at her. He sat beside her on her couch and spoke softly.

"I'm sorry, Maya. I know one day I might regret this. And, believe me, I know I'll never find anyone to put up with me the way you did. No one will deal with all my weird quirks. But I can't do what you want. I'm too screwed up. I won't make a good husband, not the way you want," he confessed.

Tears formed in her eyes and Ashok hurriedly got up to leave. His visit was brief and he had stayed for less than half an hour. The door shut behind him and it was the last time that Maya would ever see him.

CHAPTER 7

It was two years since Ashok and Maya had split up, and during this time, Sumi had gotten engaged to Surin, her longtime boyfriend of eight years. Sumi confided to Maya and Toni that she was now ready to have a family, and believed that Surin would make a good choice. She confessed that it wasn't fireworks or deep love she felt for Surin, but she knew that he would be a good provider for her and their future children. She was thirty-six years old and wanted to have at least two kids, and so as far as she was concerned, now was the time to start. Maya was surprised that Sumi had pulled the trigger, as she knew Sumi's life was busy and she had been milking the social life in Manhattan. Her career was also on a roll. Sumi was notorious for setting up social events at the latest and trendiest bars in Manhattan. Both Maya and Toni had reaped the benefits of having a friend who was a currency trader and constantly going out on the town. During the week, they were invited to have social drinks with the various traders from the investment banks that Sumi did business with. It was a very close-knit industry, and Maya and Toni often met the same dealers and traders each week. It was easy to see why Sumi was constantly invited for drinks and dinner. Although she was one of the few females in the industry, she was a very confident and successful trader. Wall Street was still very male dominated, especially investment banking; however, if you had a reputation of making money in your profession, you were looked up to and people sought you out to exchange information and discuss ideas. Sumi, also being a cool and very beautiful girl , had no problem attracting male attention and all of the salespeople constantly wined and dined her in the hopes of having business directed their way. Maya admired her friend greatly; she had the stamina to entertain her clients into the early hours of the morning as well as put up with all of the pressures that came from being in a trading and sales environment. Both Maya and Toni loved the social scene in Manhattan, especially hanging out with Sumi and her colleagues at the hippest, newest bars and lounges in the city. Maya recalled many a time when Sumi was intoxicated around her work friends who already were inebriated. The traders were loud and for the most part, pretty obnoxious. But both Maya and Toni enjoyed themselves, as the men were, for the most part, pretty harmless and not to mention, a lot of fun. They were constantly jesting and making fun of each other and were out simply to have a good time. They bought drinks "on the house" for the girls, and although Toni could hold her own, Maya was a different matter. Being a petite girl, she could really only have one or two drinks and so she usually indulged in a cocktail or a glass of red wine. Sumi was a different story. There were days when Sumi was so hung over, she would have three or four hours of sleep and report to work the next morning in a daze. Her report time was seven am, as management expected the traders to begin before the start of a new trading day. Often, Sumi would confide to Maya that she was sure she would be fired due to all of the late mornings that she arrived to work. But Sumi was extremely adept and skillful at her trade, and continuously over the years made large sums of money for the bank, so instead of being fired, she was eventually promoted to being a proprietary trader for the bank.

And now, Sumi at thirty-six years old, the biological clock had set in and she announced to her friends that she was now ready to marry her long-time boyfriend, Surin. Maya was happy for her friend; at least Sumi knew what she wanted and was ready to start a new phase in her life. The wedding was a beautiful ceremony that took place in Sumi's hometown of Brampton, Ontario, in an Indian banquet hall. Maya and Toni walked alongside Sumi as her best friends, along with a few of her younger female cousins. The silk saris they wore were heavy and exquisite, and patterned in bright colors such as yellow, turquoise and magenta, in contrast to Sumi's deep red, traditional color. The red color is the tradition of Hindu brides and Sumi looked beautiful in the red and gold ordaining her wedding sari. Sumi and Sirin walked around the fire seven times as a symbol of their new life together, with the priest translating the Sanskrit words in

English so that the entire audience would understand the vows that the couple was taking. The wedding reception was full of great food, drinks and dancing.

Sumi and Surin were moving to Philadelphia shortly after their marriage, and Maya knew she would miss Sumi's lively chatter and companionship. And recently, Toni had announced that she was moving into a West Village apartment with her new girlfriend of six months. It seemed like everyone was moving on and Maya sighed. She hoped that one day it would all come together for her as well.

Over the next two years, Maya couldn't shake off the memories of Ashok. She went over and over in her mind whether things may have been different had she been more patient. Had she forced the issue too early? Would he have committed in the end?

Her friends had all told her that Ashok was too much of a commitment-phobe to marry and that she would have been wasting her time. They believed he would have made her wait forever with no indication of any commitment. And besides, they believed he had been selfish. Maya knew she had been much more giving in the relationship than he had been and she had put up with a lot more of his idiosyncrasies. She had loved him, but that clearly wasn't enough to make it work. He had been so moody throughout their relationship and she wondered if theirs would have been an equal partnership. Deep down inside, she knew she would have been the one to adapt to his moodiness. But she had been willing to marry him despite all of his quirks. In her mind, no one was perfect and Ashok was a good man, a family man, with honest, hardworking values.

Approximately six months after the breakup, Maya met a nice Indian gentleman at a charity fundraiser for Parkinson's. His name was Rohan and he appeared to be a very refined and proper gentleman. He had been born and raised in India until the age of twenty-one, when after graduating from Delhi University, he had lived and traveled extensively abroad. His work had primarily taken him to Latin American countries such as Brazil and Mexico where he had become fluent in Spanish. He was worldly and gracious, as well as being a very successful entrepreneur in a small Internet company. He lived on the Upper East Side in Manhattan and was very interested in getting to know Maya. Thus, Maya started spending much of her free time with him and while there was not the same connection she had felt for Ashok, she enjoyed his company. His parents lived in India, but Rohan had several cousins in New York and was close to all of them. Maya eventually met with all of Rohan's cousins and they were warm and fun to be with as well. Maya and Rohan had known each other for several months and Rohan had not hit on Maya even once. It seemed to Maya that Rohan was waiting for her to show signs of romantic interest. However, as that did not occur, their relationship developed into a platonic friendship. There had been some awkward moments, especially when Maya caught Rohan gazing fondly at her over dinner when she had dressed up and worn a new outfit on a couple of occasions. Rohan's family had come to know her, and as Maya had grown fond of them, she wished deep down inside that she could have developed feelings for Rohan. Since Maya did not have siblings growing up, she was envious of Rohan's circle of cousins. What a difference there was when you had a warm, loving family around you to rely on. It would be so nice to have that in your life. But she asked herself over and over, *how could she marry someone who made you feel comfortable, who you could be yourself with, but who didn't ignite the passion in you or the desire to be kissed?* It was unfortunate, since it was clear that Rohan was the commitment type; he wanted to settle down and she knew deep down inside that he would make a good husband and father.

CHAPTER 8

Maya was thirty-nine years old and the planets had still not aligned for her in terms of love and commitment. On a lazy Sunday afternoon in Central Park, she was playing tennis with one of her best male friends, Sam, an American-born desi whom she had met a year after her move to Manhattan. It was unbelievable where the time went; Maya couldn't believe it had been almost ten years since she had moved to the Big Apple. Maya and Sam had connected instantly through a social tennis club. In addition to being a great tennis match for her on the courts, Sam had a hilarious sense of humor that kept Maya laughing till her sides hurt. She often wondered why Sam was still single at thirty-two years old, as, in her mind, he was a very good catch for a girl. He had simply said that he wanted to marry and spend his life with an Indian girl, but hadn't yet met the right person. Although he had dated many girls, none of them met his criteria for a lasting relationship. He had grown up in small, close-knit Gujarati family and was an only child.

As usual, Sam and Maya had brunch after their tennis match and caught up on their respective work, family and love lives.

"I think fate and timing has a lot to do with marriage." Sam was a very practical person. He had studied astrology in his childhood and read horoscopes for a hobby. "I told you your marriage would be delayed; your planet is in the seventh house, which means you face obstacles in your romantic life. Maybe it wouldn't be a bad idea to see an Indian astrologer. I know of one in Jackson Heights."

"Are you serious? How do you know about him?" Maya was skeptical.

"His name is Chandra Swami and he is on a local TV station. He prepares astrological charts and reads the future. He helped my cousin, Subash, find a job within a couple of months after he was laid off. Subash was unemployed for over six months and the Swami told him that he would get a job very soon if Subash did certain prayers. And then he ended up finding a job two months later.

Sam was a big believer in fate and luck. He had grown up studying astrology and was fascinated by the astrological readings of famous people who experienced not just fame, but personal tragedies, such as divorcing twice or losing a loved one to cancer. He didn't believe that everyone who claimed to foretell the future actually could, but he did believe that there were certain yogis or priests who did exude such powers. He had heard uncanny stories from his uncles and grandparents who were also believers, as they had had successful predictions in their own lives regarding death, marriage and financial matters.

"Ok, maybe I will go see him; what do I have to lose?" Maya sighed. She felt like she had waited all of her life to have normal things. She had simple wishes, just to raise a family of her own with the right person. Maybe this Swami would have some insight.

She called the Swami's office the next day and made the appointment for the following weekend. The receptionist asked for her birth date, time and place of birth. She explained that Chandra Swami would prepare her astrological chart, read Maya's past and then be able to tell her what was in store for her future.

When Maya arrived at Chandra Swami's office, she saw ten to twelve people in the small waiting area and after paying a fee of one hundred dollars to the receptionist, joined them to sit down and wait for her turn. When she was beckoned to go into the Swami's office, she saw a very small grey-haired man in his mid-fifties with a long string of beads in his hand. He also had a longish tail of hair at the back of his neck, which gave the impression of a pony tail. He nodded at her and waved his hand, beckoning for her to sit across the desk from him. In his broken English he said, "Please place your hands and touch the beads in my hand." Maya did as he requested, and after a few seconds, he withdrew his hand, turned around and started to count the beads silently. He looked at her when he was finished and said, "Your family upbringing was somewhat broken and troubled. But I see you with many close friends and it appears you have done a lot of traveling. Also, in the future, I see you will buy property. You have been successful in your career, but not so successful in love. I see a stumbling block; someone has placed black magic on you so you cannot find your marriage partner until this is cured. Someone who was jealous of you a long time ago when you were only a child has done this."

Maya looked at him blankly. She did not have two clues as to how someone had placed a curse on her; why would anyone want to do that? "So is there a cure?" She felt a bit foolish in even asking the question.

"Not to worry, I will help you. Take this lemon and make sure you burn it when you get home. I want you to recite this mantra for the next ninety days, for twenty minutes a day. Do not skip a day and pronounce this exactly as I am saying it.

"Om Aim Harim Kalim Chamunda Vichay."

The Swami pronounced each word slowly in order that Maya could repeat after him. She did so hesitantly, and after several frustrating attempts, Chandra Swami was satisfied with her pronunciation.

"Good; after ninety days, the curse will be lifted. Anytime after this period, you will be able to find your marriage partner. You will meet someone within the next year or two and have a successful marriage. But you cannot miss one day of saying the mantra; it is very important."

Maya nodded. Who could argue with the Swami? If that was what he wanted her to do, she would do it. The spiritual elements were not something Maya had explored greatly but somehow she felt this small man must have some sort of extraordinary insight, as he clearly had a following, judging by the number of people in the waiting room.

"And I want you to visit the temple once a month and pray to Mother Durga for prosperity and a family of your own. Please take a dozen red roses as offerings with you."

"What does Mother Durga signify?" asked Maya.

"She is the goddess with eight arms who has a history of killing demons and evil that lurks and surrounds all. Here, take this photo and have her image in front of you when you recite the mantra." Swami handed her a picture of a beautiful female creature on a tiger with eight arms and different weapons held in each.

"Thank you, Swamiji." Maya rose to leave and took the lemon with her and when she boarded the E train to return home to Manhattan, she felt a bit dazed. Would she be the laughingstock of her friends when she told them what had just happened? Upon her return to her small apartment on the Upper West, she promptly called her friend Sam who knew about her visit and was excited to hear how it had gone.

"Well, he told me to chant this mantra for ninety days and visit the temple once a month. And he said someone placed a curse on me," Maya skeptically said to Sam.

"I don't know about this curse, Maya, but I know meditation works and you can use this mantra to meditate on. He knows what he is talking about; he does this for a living. Anyway, what harm can come from it?" Sam said.

He himself was a spiritual person and cared about his friends and family greatly.

"You're right. I'll try it," said Maya. Sam was the only person she spoke to about her visit to Swami Ji, as Sam believed in the mystical powers of the universe and she knew had she spoken to any of her other friends about this she would have been made a laughingstock. So Maya followed Sam's advice and kept the secret between the two of them.

Over the next three months, Maya would recite the mantra for twenty minutes in the mornings after showering. The photo of Mother Durga was always in front of her when she meditated, and over time, Maya started to feel a sense of peace after her meditations. She also visited the temple once a month, as she had promised Chandra Swami and took offerings, such as red roses to place in front of the idol that resembled the female Goddess, Mother Durga. Her curiosity about the Hindu religion had heightened and she would often find herself in the Barnes and Noble bookstore at the corner of 66th and Broadway, pouring over religious books about the Ramayana and the Bhaghvad Gita. She had never been religious as a child growing up, as her mother was not a devout Christian and her father had not instilled any Hindu beliefs on her, as he himself was agnostic. But Maya had been a spiritual child and believed innately that good came to those who did good deeds, and what goes around eventually comes around. She became more learned about the Hindu religion, its spiritual laws of karma and dharma, and teachings of how to live life purely without any material gain. It was fascinating to read the numerous myths and stories that embodied its religious history, each one having a moral lesson to teach about human principles and values.

CHAPTER 9

It was a dark, thunderous night on a Saturday in mid-April and as Maya looked out at her apartment window, she saw the lightning flashes reflect on the moving branches of the trees outside. She shivered; it always made her a bit nervous to hear the loud, thunderous noises and hoped there would be no damage caused by the storm. She was waiting in her apartment for Sumi to arrive. Sumi had called that afternoon and had been hysterical on the phone. The only thing that Maya had gathered from her was that Surin and she had gotten into a nasty fight, and Sumi needed to leave and spend the night away from their home. Sumi wanted to take the first train to Manhattan from Philadelphia, and Maya had agreed to see her, so she was patiently waiting for Sumi to arrive.

Her internal building phone rang and the concierge announced her. "Ma'am, I have a Sumi downstairs."

Maya opened the door to greet a very teary eyed and

71

drenched Sumi. She was wearing a wet, bright yellow raincoat and rubber boots and was carrying a small suitcase in one hand. She started sobbing and Maya took her suitcase, while Sumi took off her raincoat and boots.

"Maya, he's gone. I don't know where he is..." Sumi was hysterical now, and Maya hugged her friend, trying to make sense of what was going on. They sat down on the couch and Sumi poured out her story in between tears.

"We've been fighting. I've been working terribly long hours, sometimes I haven't come home until nine or ten o'clock, and Surin would be home waiting. He gets off at six every day and when I got home the other night, he was sprawled on the couch, watching TV, and I lost it. I work so hard every night and all I asked was that he picks up a few things for the house and, of course, he hasn't done anything, so there's nothing for me to eat. He's lying there, watching TV, and says he's tired; he hasn't cooked dinner and there are no groceries in the house. And on top of that, I haven't been able to get pregnant and we've been trying for so long and nothing's happened. The doctors say it's just a matter of time, that there's nothing wrong with him or me. And I can't help but wonder if it's me or him, I don't know which one, or if it's that we just need to give it more time. I know eight months isn't forever. But I'm stressed about my job and why I'm not conceiving, so I end up yelling at him, sometimes for no reason, just because I'm irritated. I've been yelling at him every night for the past two weeks. My job is so demanding and Surin doesn't get it; he complains that I work too hard. And he says he hardly sees me. What does he want me to do, quit? He only earns half of what I make and he knows how important my career is. He knew that when we got married. We had such a big fight the other day; he resents my hours at work and says we hardly make love anymore. I told him that it's not easy working the type of job that I have and I'm exhausted. I told him to pull his weight around the house, and then I took a fit and told him he wasn't the same person that I loved and married. He was so hurt and didn't even come into the bedroom. He slept on the couch and when I got home last night, he wasn't there. He left a note for me on the kitchen table. He wrote that he had fallen out of love with me and he couldn't take it anymore. He also said that I shouldn't bother contacting him. How can I contact him when I don't even know where he went? He won't answer his cell and respond to my emails." Sumi was hysterical now and was gasping for air.

Maya handed her a glass of water. "It's okay, Sumi. He'll come back, don't worry."

"I've contacted everyone that knows him, but his parents and sister won't tell me where he is. I'm going to show up at his office on Monday; he has to be there," Sumi said.

"Calm down, honey, don't do anything too rash. I think you should take some time. Take a deep breath and just relax. It will be fine," Maya said in a reassuring voice.

Sumi sipped the glass of water and proceeded to talk for the next three hours, pouring out the details of her relationship with Surin; she confessed to treating him subserviently. There were many a time that she had accused him of not being well read, unlike the smart Wall Street colleagues she had kept company with over the years. And she confessed to picking on him and yelling at him frequently during the year they lived together in Philadelphia. How she had lost respect for him and felt that his job as a computer specialist did not compare to her career as an analyst at the private equity firm she had joined. They had started trying to have kids soon after they were married, but it hadn't happened even after eight months, and the stress had adversely affected Sumi and her moods. She also confessed that it had been wrong for her to cheat on him during her single years in Manhattan, while he was patiently waiting for her to commit. It was a profound and confessional time for Sumi. She was always so confident about her abilities and keeping the balance of her job, family and love life. Maya had never seen Sumi so broken and hard on herself. All Sumi wanted was her life back with Surin, and she wanted the chance to show Surin that she was still the woman that he had loved and married. But Sumi knew deep down inside that she had to do some changing as well. She had said some pretty harsh words to her husband. The guilt and remorse she was feeling for how she had treated her husband was weighing on her heavily, and it had taken Surin walking out on her to realize how important their marriage was. She knew she would do whatever it took to save their marriage. She was married and the vows she had spoken were the most important thing in her life. And she would do whatever it took to salvage it. Through this experience, she realized how much she loved Surin and needed him. He had been there for her for so many years, her sounding board, always encouraging her career and her aspirations in life. Where would she ever find a man like him again? He was so patient and supportive of her, in every aspect of her life. He had been the one to encourage her to move to Manhattan when she had received the offer from Deutsche Bank. He had been the one to console her when she was frustrated with her bosses or coworkers. And now she had taken him for granted and treated him like a doormat. It was no wonder he had reached his limit. She had pushed him too far and she knew that she would take back the awful things she had said to him if she could. It was a good lesson for her. Everyone had their limitations, and relationships were so fragile. But Sumi was determined to find a way to convince him to give them a second chance, and she prayed to God that Surin would be willing to give their marriage another chance.

The next day, Maya and Sumi walked through Central Park, reminiscing about their lives together. As Maya bid her weeping girlfriend goodbye at the train station, she assured her that her marriage was going to be alright. Deep down inside, she hoped that she was right and that Sumi would be able to convince Surin to take her back.

The weeks flew by and Sumi called Maya every day to talk to her about her marriage with Surin. It had taken an entire week before Sumi even heard from Surin, and then he had finally agreed to meet her, after hours and days of Sumi pleading with him on the phone to give it a chance. But Surin was not that easy to convince, having been through a lot of soul-searching in terms of what he wanted from their marriage. He related that he was going away for two weeks; in fact, he had booked a hiking trek through the Himalayas with a tour group that he had found on the Internet. He needed to get away to clear his mind and do something different. He told Sumi that he would be in touch with her after his trip and they would talk about things afterwards. Sumi was shocked; she begged Surin not to leave at such a critical juncture in their marriage, but Surin had made up his mind. He was unyielding and told her that he needed this time and space away from her. And he wanted to do something adventurous like this where he would be away from it all, and be able to find a clear perspective on things. Sumi respected his love for adventure and hiking, but told him the timing was terrible. She wanted him to work on their marriage, not run away from it. But Surin didn't agree and was firm in his decision to spend time away.

Maya knew this was the hardest time in Sumi's life, and she listened endlessly for hours to her pain and suffering on the phone. She was reassuring and optimistic, and told Sumi that she really believed that Surin loved her and would make it work. Sumi would just have to be patient now and wait for Surin to arrive back with a clear head.

The next two weeks were the most bittersweet of Sumi's life. Surin had left for his hiking trip and Sumi just didn't get why he would choose to go away at this time. She anxiously awaited his return. And as luck would have it, during the time that he was away, she made a shocking discovery.

As soon as she found out, she called Maya to break the news.

"Maya, I can't believe it. I'm pregnant," Sumi said

"What?" Maya was shocked as well. She couldn't believe that it had happened right after Surin had left.

"I am so happy and so sad at the same time. My period was late this week, and I just got back from the doctor's, who confirmed the blood test. My husband should be the first to know the news and yet I haven't heard from him in over a week," Sumi said sadly.

"I know, but you will. He's back in a week and this news is awesome. This is what you both wanted. It will work out for sure now. He'll be so thrilled. " Maya was happy for her friend and very reassuring.

Sumi was expecting for Surin to arrive back in a week from his Himalayan hiking trip, but he never did arrive. He didn't call on the day he was supposed to be back. Sumi frantically called his parents in Toronto and learned that they hadn't heard from him either. His father was worried as well. He had called the airline that Surin was scheduled to fly back on and discovered that his son had not been on it. He then tracked down the travel agency that had booked Surin's tour package, but they could not tell him why Surin had not been on the flight back. Apparently, all of the others in the tour group had arrived safely back. Surin's parents were very worried and Sumi was hysterical. She had told them the news of her pregnancy a few days after she had found out and they had been thrilled. They had then opened up to her and reassured her of Surin's love and his commitment to their marriage. They told her that they never doubted of his eventual return to her.

The day after Surin was expected to arrive back, Sumi received a phone call from the head of the Himalayas tour group. It was bad news. Surin had disappeared. The last day of their hike, Surin had separated from the rest of the group unbeknownst to them, and he had slipped on a large boulder on a very steep climb. When the tour guide had called his name, he had not responded and the group had stalled their hike for hours, searching for him. They had called for a helicopter to help locate him, and unfortunately, the rescue team was not able to find him either. The helicopter had flown around for hours that night, but no one had been visible. Surin was declared "missing" in the Himalayas and no one had any idea whether he was dead or alive.

Maya's heart ached for her best friend. It was hard enough that Sumi had been so hard on Surin during their marriage, but for her to lose him like this. It was a tragedy of epic proportions. And a newborn had been conceived just before Surin had left. The irony was not lost on Sumi, the fact that they hadn't gotten pregnant in so long was what had precipitated and caused the stress that their marriage had undergone.

The grief that overcame Sumi after learning of Surin's disappearance seemed unbearable. But Sumi knew that there was much more at stake now. She was going to have a child who would need and depend on her. After much reflection, Sumi decided to relocate back to Toronto where she would have the support of her own parents and in-laws. Luckily, her company had an office in Toronto where they were willingly to relocate her. So, Sumi moved back home to Toronto in her parent's home, where she carried out the rest of her pregnancy to term and delivered a beautiful baby girl. She named her Lori Lee, which had been the name Surin had picked for a girl. He was still declared missing and under the laws, a husband was declared dead after one year of not being heard from or found. It was a traumatic time for Sumi and it would be years before she stopped blaming herself for Surin being "missing." But she found solace in her baby, Lorilee, who became the apple of her eye. She had her daughter, at least, who for many years to come, would be the center of her world. There was nothing like being a mother. Sumi had always dreamed of being one, and now, at least, she would have her daughter in life.

CHAPTER 10

On the Memorial Day weekend of 2008, Maya decided to visit Toronto. She was staying with one of her oldest and dearest friends, Ida. They had spent all Saturday of that weekend visiting Sumi and spending time with her one–year-old daughter, Lorilee, who was a spitting image of Surin. Both families had now accepted the fact that he may never be back and had focused their attention on raising Lorilee, who was now crawling forwards and backwards and attempting to walk at the same time. Maya had a wonderful time with Sumi and Lorilee, who had become her goddaughter and whom she loved and spoiled generously.

The next day, on Sunday afternoon, Maya and Ida strolled through downtown Toronto, shopping. They were waiting in line to order coffee and doughnuts at Tim Hortons in the Eaton Center mall when Maya's cell phone rang. Maya quickly picked up without looking at the number.

"Hello, this is Roman calling. Is Maya there?

"Speaking, who is this?" Maya didn't recognize the name or the number.

"Hi, I got your number from your real estate agent, Anna. Did she tell you I would be calling?"

"Oh, yes, of course! Sorry, I am actually in Toronto, can I get back to you tomorrow when I am back home?"

"Sure," Roman said.

Maya hung up and laughed. While sipping a hot Tim Hortons' coffee and munching on a double chocolate frosted doughnut, she told her story to Ida.

"You wouldn't believe who is setting me up? Anna, my real estate agent. Remember she helped me look for condos?" Maya was proud of her condo purchase, it had happened last year when her landlady had called to let her know that she and her husband had decided to get divorced, and that she was listing the condo where Maya lived for sale. Coincidentally, Maya had decided to engage a real estate agent to help her look for a property, having done fairly well at her job as a research analyst at Bearings Bank over the past ten years. She and Anna, her broker, had seen over twenty apartments together in the city, but Maya hadn't found the right one. Either the apartments were too expensive or were not in the right location, or she hadn't liked the layout. Maya's break came when her landlady called her to inform her that she needed to sell the condo that Maya was renting from her. Since Maya was interested in buying a place, they had negotiated a deal together. Fortunately, she had been able to strike a price incredibly under market, as her landlady had needed to raise cash very quickly. Maya was thrilled over the deal she had struck, but unfortunately had to tell Anna the news that she was no longer in the market. She and Anna had gotten along famously, and despite not having been able to sell Maya a property, she had generously offered to set her up with a nice gentleman, who was also one of her clients.

"Roman's divorced and has two little girls," Maya told Ida.

"Wow, are you okay with that? I'm not sure I would be ready for kids. Are you?" Ida said. She was thirty-nine years old, a year younger than Maya and was still waiting for her Prince Charming as well.

"I know it's not ideal, but I'm forty years old now, and who knows, what if I can't have kids of my own?" Maya said ruefully. She knew she had to be more realistic about the men that were out there, especially at her age. She hadn't dated anyone with children, but didn't want to prejudge anyone just because they had been divorced. Unfortunately, as she knew from her own experience, children of divorced parents went through a lot of trauma, and she had ample empathy for their innocence. Although it wasn't her first choice, Maya didn't feel that she could afford to be that picky given her age, and therefore was open to the idea of meeting someone with children.

The day after Maya returned to Manhattan, she left a message on Roman's voicemail and surprisingly, his response was very quick. The next day, during her lunch hour, she received a text from him on her cell phone.

"Would you like to meet for drinks tonight?" Maya responded in the affirmative and they both agreed to meet downtown at the Tribecca Grand Hotel later that evening.

Maya was twenty minutes late, and when she approached the hotel bar, her eyes caught those of a distinguished-looking man who had a streak of silver running through his thick, jet black hair. He was wearing dark-rimmed preppy glasses and had very smooth, baby-like skin that made him seem so much younger than his age, which she knew to be in his early forties.

They both ordered a couple of glasses of red wine, and Roman and Maya spent the next three hours chatting and learning about each other. Maya learned he was a banker with a prestigious British bank in the city and that he was divorced for three years from an American woman, with whom he had two young girls, aged six and eight. He saw his girls every other weekend and he loved being with them. He said he was ready to marry again, but only to the right person. He was in no rush to repeat his first experience that had obviously not gone well for him. She learned that his parents lived in Bangalore, India, and that he had made a vow to visit them every year. While Roman spoke about his background, Maya immediately felt that there was something different about him. He was kind and spoke so honestly; she knew he was genuine and wasn't into the game playing that so many single bachelors in the city engaged in. He didn't seem flaky or flighty either. Roman was Ivy League educated and he held a complicated job in finance on Wall Street. It was obvious that he was brilliant in his field, yet he appeared so modest about his own abilities and successes. They talked about finance on Wall Street, and what a tumultuous time it was for bankers given the massive losses faced by investment banks, and the numerous consolidations taking place in the industry. Some of the largest banks in the country were failing and merging together and it was a time like no other. Many firms were downsizing and people were nervous about their jobs, especially on Wall Street. The economy was on the brink of collapse, and both Roman and Maya felt very fortunate that they were still employed during this time. The evening ended around ten o'clock and Roman walked outside and hailed a cab for Maya. He kissed her on her cheek and suggested that they meet again soon. When Maya arrived home, she fell into a very restful sleep, with a warm feeling in her heart.

The next couple of months were an exciting time for both Maya and Roman. They spent as much time together as possible. They discovered a sweet type of passion filled with kindness and mutual love. Roman found Maya very sexy; he often told her that she was unlike any woman he had known. He worshipped her body and loved her sense of humor. Maya was always excited to see Roman, and her heart always felt a flutter prior to meeting him. The physical chemistry between them was perfect. The first time he made love to her was gentle and slow, and lasted for what seemed like an eternity. He was eager to please her, and would place soft kisses all over her body and massage her breasts tenderly. They spent hours touching and caressing each other's bodies before culminating their passion with the final act. He would then cup her breasts with his hands and kiss her nipples, arousing them sensuously with his tongue. She was so petite and slim under his long and muscular frame. He loved the large, full breasts under her petiteness, and loved watching her climax before satisfying himself. Roman was the most perfect lover Maya had known and she was so easily aroused by his touch, evidenced by her wetness below. Each time they met, their lovemaking grew more intense and passionate.

Roman and Maya were in love. They shared many common interests. Both liked similar cuisines and enjoyed eating out, yet were also comfortable in making simple dishes at home. The first time Maya cooked for Roman, she had made a curry chicken dish with rice pilaf, and Roman was amazed. He loved the fact that she enjoyed cooking and knew how to do it well. He told her that no woman had ever cooked for him like she did. He was not so handy in the kitchen, but Maya didn't mind. After enjoying a home-cooked meal at Maya's place, they would take long walks in Central Park and usually ended up at an independent ice cream shop on the corner of 79th and Amsterdam. The lineups were long, as it was very popular in the summertime. Roman's favorite dessert was the Caramel and Moose print ice cream, which he generously shared with Maya. And on the weekends, when Maya would stay over at Roman's home across the Hudson River, they would often drive down to the Jersey Shore to Long Branch Beach. Both Roman and Maya enjoyed the long strolls along the shoreline, and had deep conversations about their childhood and different places where they had traveled. Maya learned that Roman had lived in the Philippines for several years when he had been a small child. He was only ten years old at the time, but had very distinct memories of it. His father, who had been retired for the past five years, had worked for the Indian government as an engineer. His work travels had taken him and his family throughout India, as well as abroad, before settling down permanently in Bangalore. Roman's father was a very smart man and had done extremely well for himself in both real estate and investments. Roman's mother was a very religious and traditional lady, and although Roman respected and loved his parents, they had grown somewhat apart. He had adopted more liberal views from the Western culture, which differed greatly from their conservative ones. Roman had one sister who was slightly elder than him and she was busy raising three young boys in Washington, DC. It was his sister that had brought Roman to the US, as she had convinced her professor at Ohio State that her younger brother was a very smart boy and would do well here. Thus, Roman at eighteen years old was given the chance to come to America and make a name for himself.

Maya and Roman shared similar interests in movies, and also frequently watched the business channels, as both were in finance and followed the markets. Their political views did not always mesh, but Maya enjoyed the debates they would have and always respected Roman's opinions, even if she didn't always agree with him.

Maya found herself alone on the alternate weekends when Roman was occupied with his two little girls. Although he always called her to say good morning or goodnight during that period, she still felt lonely without him. It was a hard adjustment to make when she had just finished spending a lovely, romantic time with him over one weekend, and then to be alone again the following weekend. She hinted to him every so often that she would love to meet his girls, and Roman said that he would do so when the time was right and when he was sure that Maya would be a permanent part of his life. He was very protective of his young daughters and didn't want them to exposed to any of the women he was dating until there was a permanent commitment. He knew his daughters and how sensitive and vulnerable they were, especially at such young ages. Maya understood. She recalled the days herself when she was a young girl, when her parents were in the midst of their divorce. Meeting her stepmother, Sheela, for the first time had been a very hard experience for her. And now she had come full circle. For the first time, she understood what Sheela had felt while she was dating her father and anticipating meeting her. She had a newfound appreciation for her stepmother. It was now her turn to be the patient one, while dating Roman and waiting to meet his kids.

Chapter 11

Roman and Maya had been dating for seven months. On a lazy Sunday afternoon, when they were entangled in each other's arms, Roman broke the news to her.

"I have something to tell you." He said seriously.

"Hope it's good news," she responded, running a finger down his long, bare chest.

"My company is transferring me to Texas. I requested it because the kids are moving there. Remember my ex-wife remarried a few months back? Her husband is moving to Dallas, and I can't live without my kids, Maya. So I have to do the right thing and move close to them."

"How can you do that? Can't you just visit them? I don't understand. How can you uproot your whole life and me? What about us?" Maya was shocked and upset.

"They're only six and eight years old. I can't just fly there every two weeks. I don't have a home for them to come visit me. So I need to be near my kids. They still go to school and I need to help them with their school work and attend their soccer games. I want to watch them grow up," Roman said matter-of-factly.

"And we can still see each other. You can fly to see me when I don't have the kids, or once a month, I'll fly back here. We'll make it work," he continued calmly.

Maya felt like shrieking. When would she get a break and have a relationship work out smoothly for a change?

"I don't see how, Roman. Your life will be so far away. And you see the kids twice a month. That is in your divorce agreement. So how is it possible that you'll still have time for me? When did you request your company to transfer you?"

"A couple of weeks ago, but I didn't want to tell you until I knew for certain that the firm would be able to move me. I have mixed feelings about it. I don't want to leave New York, but I want to see and be near my kids. On the other hand, I don't want to leave you either, but we can still see each other and make it work."

Maya shook her head. "No, Roman, this isn't what I want. I thought you really loved me. But the fact that you can pick up to be near your kids and just want a long distance relationship after the past seven months — that's not what I'm looking for at this stage in my life." Tears flowed down her cheeks. She knew this was the beginning of the end. She could recognize the signs clearly.

Roman spent the next couple of hours trying to convince her to give it a try. But Maya was stubborn. She would rather let go and cut her losses than hang onto a thread of hope. She had already been down this road before. Long distance had been tough with Ashok. They had taken a year to really get to know and fall in love with each other, as the distance involved a lot of flying back and forth, scheduling time and communicating by telephone. That had been hard enough. But this was different. She and Roman had spent an enormous amount of time together over the past seven months. They already knew each other well. She didn't understand how he could ask her to do a long distance relationship when he claimed to love her. She made up her mind. She didn't want to be vulnerable again. She wanted to be with the man she loved at a moment's notice, not at the whim of flights and travel plans. How could he ask her of this, especially when there was no mention of a commitment from Roman? Had their last seven months together meant so little to him that he couldn't even discuss his plans with her? Maya wished Roman would have brought up something, such as getting engaged or married, talking about their future together, anything to show that he was committed. But there was no talk of what their future was. How could he simply leave and throw this at her, and inform her that he was moving on. He hadn't even included her in the decision. It made her realize that he still wasn't ready for more. She knew it was a big step, to make a commitment, since he had kids and had suffered from a bad marriage. He said he loved her, but what did that mean when he could just pick up and leave? And she felt that he should have shown her the respect to talk and work things out together. To make long-term plans without including her simply hurt.

"We are finished, Roman. It's over. I don't want to do

long distance. There's no commitment here. And you are willing to move to another city without even discussing it with me first. I understand you want to be close to your girls, but our relationship is clearly not a priority for you. So I don't think we should communicate after this. We both have to move on," Maya said firmly. Her heart was breaking inside but she knew she had to do this. The last thing she wanted was to be strung along again. She was done with the conversation as well as their relationship.

The next couple of months for Maya were very difficult, to say the least. Roman had moved to Dallas, Texas, and although he attempted to contact her, she refused to take his calls or answer any of his emails. She had meant what she said. She loved Roman and he was a man like no one she had ever met. But she was so adamant. She knew herself and if she let herself fall into the same trap of falling more deeply in love with a man who couldn't put their relationship first, it would be the most painful process to recover from. Her heart was empty and Maya threw herself into her work. She had social invitations to attend charity events, join friends for drinks and kept busy with business dinners. Time flew by, but there was emptiness in her heart that had been left by Roman's departure. The memories of their love and times together were engrained in her heart. When she woke up in the morning, his image was the first thing she saw, and the last before she fell asleep at night.

It was May 2009 and exactly a year since she had met Roman. It had been four months since he had left for Texas, and Maya was thinking of their first date together when she got a call from her stepfather, Giuseppe.

"Maya, I have some bad news. Your mom is really sick. She has been ill for over a month, but we didn't know why so we didn't tell you, as we didn't wish to worry you. But she has gotten worse now. She has leukemia."

"What?" Maya was shocked. "When and how did it happen?"

"We don't know how, but she was starting to feel very weak, a month back and had gone to see the doctor for several tests. We got the results back after a few weeks. And they confirmed a tumor. It was malignant. She's strong but her spirits are really down. It's hit her really hard." Giuseppe sounded sad and his voice broke while he was speaking.

"Oh my God, can you please put her on the phone," Maya said

"She's in the hospital right now for more tests. She'll be there overnight. She asked me to call you," Giuseppe said

"I'm taking the first flight out," Maya said. She scrambled to get her Blackberry and sent a quick note to her boss, saying she would need to take a couple of days off, as her mother was seriously ill.

The flight back to Charlottetown on that Saturday night was a difficult one. Her heart was full of trepidation and worry. The mother who had raised her was seriously ill in a hospital bed. She prayed that her mom would be strong and recover quickly. Leukemia was a devastating disease. How could Natasha have gotten cancer? She had been so healthy and physically fit her entire life. She loved exercising and had such a good diet. What had caused this terrible growth inside her? Maya wished she knew so she could wave it away.

When Maya landed at the airport, Giuseppe was there to greet her. Together they drove straight to the hospital and when Maya saw her mom, she was shaken. The beautiful redheaded woman who had raised her lay in the hospital bed and her face was as pale as the pillow that she was lying on. Her body looked limp and frail and it was clear the disease had taken a large toll on her. Natasha started crying when she saw Maya and both mother and daughter hugged each other, as if they were each other's lifeline. The next few days, Maya stayed at the hospital, talking to Natasha throughout the day in between her chemotherapy treatments. She could see that the treatments were extremely painful and left her mother feeling very weak. Maya tried to be strong and as encouraging as she could be for her. During the nights, she would sleep in the small armchair provided in the hospital room so that she would be the first thing Natasha would see when she woke up in the mornings. Throughout the days, mother and daughter would reminisce about Maya's childhood; how she had been scared of the dark and often stole to her parent's room to cuddle with them in their bed in the middle of the night. How Maya had loved ice skating in the winter and the beavertail hot chocolate drinks afterwards. And how she had loved the woods and pretended to play student and teacher with her friends, using the thick trees as a blackboard. And how she loved the long walks on the beaches with her mother during the summer time and rolling her jean pants to her knees so she could soak her feet alongside the ocean. Natasha told her stories about her grandparents and how much they had loved Maya when they were alive, as she had been their only grandchild. She also spoke fondly of Giuseppe and how he had seen her through this trying time. He loved her and Natasha confessed that she wouldn't have been able to make it through this ordeal without him. Even though Maya didn't have great affection for him, she was glad that he had been there for her mother. Giuseppe's love had clearly been confined to Maya's mother as he had not even attempted to develop a relationship with his stepdaughter. Thus, the majority of Maya's Christmas holiday time had been spent with her Dad and Sheela. It had been clear from the start that Giuseppe tolerated her, but he had never conversed with her long enough to really get to know her. His lack of interest shortened Maya's visits with them to only two nights over the holidays. She felt far more comfortable with her father and Sheela. Maya sighed. But at least Giuseppe had been there for Natasha and was grateful for that.

The physician had diagnosed her mother with chronic leukemia and gave no indications for a timeframe for recovery. He was professional and had an excellent reputation as an oncologist. Maya prayed that he was successful in removing the cancerous cells that had spread through her mother's body. Life was so tenuous. She didn't understand how her mother, who seemed healthy all of her life, could have contracted such a terrible disease. Tears formed in her eyes. Life wasn't fair no matter how you cut it. It just comes, the good and bad, and you have to deal with the cards that life hands you.

Maya went to see her dad and Sheela before she left for her flight back to New York. The afternoon was somber as everyone was shocked by the news of her mother's cancer. It was a terrible plight for a sixty-two-year-old woman who had always appeared to be the picture of good health. Maya's dad drove her to the airport and when she arrived back in New York, it was a different period for her. For a long time to come, her mind and thoughts were full of her mom, as it was hard to focus on work. It helped to know that her mom had Giuseppe to take care of her, who was, bless his soul, her mom's anchor. Life continued the way it had been before, only with a slightly different perspective. Life could change at the turn of a corner, and Natasha's cancer caused a constant fear and worry in Maya's mind. One day, Maya hoped too that she would meet the right person, as growing old alone was a fearful prospect and the support and companionship in the later years was so important to enriching your own life.

CHAPTER 12

It was a Saturday night and the nightlife in the famous Meatpacking District was bustling with crowds, full of both locals and European tourists. Tall female Russian and French models that were notably a size zero and over five feet eight were having drinks at the famous Buddha Bar. The scene could have been out of a movie. The models were surrounded by American males who were hitting on them with the hopes of getting lucky. The huge bronze Buddha in the middle of the restaurant, with a stream of running water at its feet, marked the ambience of this glittering, loud and vibrant scene.

Maya, Toni, Sam and Rohan were enjoying a wonderful meal at the Buddha Bar in celebration of Sam's engagement to Angela. The couple had dated for a year before announcing their wedding plans. The ceremony was slated for later that year, as neither believed in long engagements. Sam had met Angela through a family friend and within a couple of months, he had fallen in love with her and she with him. Angela was a physician and a sweet girl who had a heart of gold. Maya liked her instantly and they soon became fast friends. It was heartwarming to know that one of her best male friends had chosen someone that she clicked with. Usually, her male friends had significant others who were possessive and oftentimes faded from her life due to their spouse's jealousies. She was happy that Angela treated her like a sister, as Sam was one of her dearest friends. It was too bad that Angela couldn't have joined in their celebration with Sam's friends, but she was on call. Her busy life at the hospital demanded overnight calls every weekend and as she was still a resident, Sam would have to deal with her schedule for another year.

"Are you still meditating?' Sam asked Maya.

"Well sort of. I do at times; it gives me some peace," answered Maya.

"How is your mother?" asked Toni.

"She's in remission. Thank God. I was never as scared as when I saw her lying on that hospital bed. She was so weak. But she is feeling much better now and the doctors say she is doing really well," Maya said.

"I'm so glad; that's great news. By the way, I have some news as well," Toni said

All three friends, Rohan, Sam and Maya, looked at Toni curiously. Was she going to be the next one to announce her engagement? They knew that she had been happily living together with her lover for the past few years.

"My parents met Sarah last month and they really

"Let's meet at seven pm at Serendipity," Roman wrote back.

"Okay," Maya was stumped. She couldn't believe he was here. She was probably making a mistake, but her heartstrings tugged at her. She had to see him. After work, she went home to take a quick shower and pulled out a beautiful, black v-shaped cashmere sweater and blue jeans. Her make-up was quick and simple. The lipstick was a sheer, pink gloss and she wore her eyeliner as a simple, faint line on her lower lids and with a touch of mascara, she was ready to leave. Her heart skipped a beat as she entered the doors of Serendipity.

Roman was sitting at a table in the middle of the small restaurant and there were two young girls seated in front of him. Maya was stunned. They were his daughters. She recognized them instantly from the photos he had shown her. And their resemblance to their father was striking. The elder daughter was nine and she had a beautiful angular jaw and high cheekbones with big eyes and long, dark hair. The younger was seven years old, and had a short bob hairstyle, but the same olive complexion and features as her sister. The girls could have passed for twins and Maya saw so much of Roman in them.

"Hello, Maya, how are you doing? Roman stood up to kiss her on the cheek.

He waved to his girls. "This is Tara and Rhea. Girls, say hello to Maya."

"Hello, Maya," Tara said shyly. She was the elder of the two and looked up at Maya with curiosity.

"Hello, Maya," echoed Rhea. She was more bold and stared at Maya, as if she was checking her out.

"Hi Tara and Rhea. I have heard a lot about you girls." Maya sat down next to Roman.

She was flabbergasted. Roman hadn't mentioned anything about the girls being with him. During the time she had dated him for the entire seven months, he had been gun-shy about introducing her to them.

"We're here for the week on vacation. I thought the girls might like to visit with their old friends. And I also wanted to visit with mine," Roman said, gazing at her fondly.

"That's great. I 'm glad you called. And it's really nice to finally meet your girls. How do you like your new school in Dallas?" Maya asked the girls.

For the next couple of hours, Maya was completely engrossed in learning about Rhea and Tara's big move to Dallas, and their new school and friends there. Initially, they were reserved and didn't talk much, but Maya persisted in her conversation with them, eventually drawing them out to talk and voice their thoughts and feelings. Soon enough, the girl's chatter filled the air, and they were spilling over each other to tell her stories about what they were learning in school and their likes and dislikes.

Roman watched the three of them interact and he knew in his heart then and there that he had made the wrong call. Maya was the woman he loved and had missed terribly during the six months they had been apart. He should have taken her with him to Dallas instead of leaving her here. He had been so lonely without her. Seeing her with his kids confirmed his desire to be a part of her life, and hoped that she would still want to be a part of his.

God knows she could easily be dating someone else and that it might be too late.

"Okay, kids, we have to go now. It's nine o'clock and past your bedtime," Roman said firmly. He was staying at the Hudson hotel on the Upper West Side near the Time Warner Center. Both Rhea and Tara put up a fuss. They weren't ready to call it a night, but their father was firm and so both scurried to put their coats on. They knew better than to argue when he had that tone in his voice.

"Say goodbye to Maya," Roman said to his girls.

"Goodbye, Maya," Both Rhea and Tara said in unison. They both looked up at her with their beautiful large eyes and Maya reached down to give them both a hug.

"We'll see you girls, again. It was a lot of fun getting to know you," she said to them.

All four of them walked out of the restaurant, and Roman hailed a cab for Maya.

"Can I call you tomorrow?" he whispered while kissing her on the cheek.

"Yes," Maya whispered back softly. During the ride back home, Maya's thoughts were confusing to say the least. Why was Roman here for a week and why was he introducing her to his girls? She didn't know any of the answers, but she did know that having her meet his girls was a very big step for him.

The next day, by mid-morning, Maya received another text message from Roman.

"The girls and I had a lot of fun last night. Would you mind joining us for dinner tonight?"

Maya replied back "Tonight doesn't work for me; I have a company event to attend to."

"Would tomorrow night work, then?" Roman was persistent.

"Yes, that should be fine," Maya responded. Her heart was racing. The last she wanted to do was attend a business function, but her work was also important to her and she wasn't about to miss it, especially since Roman was here for an entire week.

However, time was precious and Maya also wanted to get to know the girls. And so she cleared her calendar the rest of the week to spend time with Roman and his daughters. On Wednesday evening, the four of them went to Central Park Zoo together. Both Tara and Rhea had been there several times before, but each of the girls still loved watching their favorite animals. Tara's was the peacock; she loved how the bird spread her feathers to show off her bright blue, green and purple colors. Rhea's favorite was the giraffe; she was fascinated by the long neck and height of this creature. And at the end of the evening, both of them started imitating the animals; they were both yelling moos and neighs and seal-like sounds in competition with each other. Each girl made an animal-like noise at the top of her lungs to try to outdo her sister. Maya laughed so hard; it was a howl to hear the two girls competing.

On Thursday evening, they all went to see Enchanted, the famous Disney movie, which had some wonderful musical tunes and a plot where good conquers evil. The girls loved it and started singing along, and even Maya and Roman enjoyed the splendid fairytale that was true to its name.

It was Friday evening and Roman had dropped off the girls to a family friend's house so he could spend alone time with Maya. He had made reservations at their favorite Indian cuisine, Amma on the East side of Manhattan. They had spent Maya's birthday there and she recalled fondly how much she had enjoyed that night.

They both ordered a glass of red wine and Maya could no longer contain her curiosity.

"Roman, why did you have me meet the girls, especially since you're no longer living here? It's been so confusing for me, I don't understand. Don't get me wrong, I think they're great, I love being with them. I just don't get it." She looked at him with puzzlement.

"Maya, I've missed you. It's been tough. I never realized how much I would. I'm glad you met me again. The kids really like you. You've been so great with them."

Roman looked straight into her eyes while he spoke.

"But none of this makes any sense. You're still in Texas," Maya said.

Roman looked at her seriously.

"Not for much longer. I've thought about it a lot. When I moved, I really believed I was doing the right thing. I wanted to see my kids grow up, but I soon realized that their lives are very busy with school, and soon they are going to be teenagers and wanting to spend less time with their dad and more time with their friends. I only see them every other weekend, and during the times I don't see them, my life seems so empty. And that is when I realize how much I miss you. Maya, I've made a decision. I want to move back here to New York, if you'll have me back in your life. So I am going to ask the firm to transfer me back. And I can still fly down to see the kids on alternate weekends. They love you, Maya. When I saw you with the girls this week, I realized we could all be a family together. I was surprised to see them warm up to you so quickly. You have such a way with them. I admit I was very nervous to introduce them to you, since I wasn't sure how they would take it. And I feel so protective of them, since I know I let them down when their mom and I split up. It was heartbreaking for me to leave them and just see them every other weekend. They were so hurt by the divorce as well. I just couldn't throw another woman at them, as they love their mom so much. That's why it took me so long to introduce you. But I am glad that I finally did. Seeing you with them, Maya, makes me realize that they're not as fragile as I thought. They genuinely love being with you. You're so natural with them. And I love being with you. I was so lonely without you."

Roman went down on his hands and knees and held her hand. He dipped into his pocket and brought out the most beautiful, sparkling solitaire diamond ring set in a princess cut. He held it out to her. "I love you, Maya. Will you marry me?"

Maya gasped and tears formed in her eyes. She was stunned and there were no words that came out. She couldn't speak.

"Please, say something," Roman whispered.

"Yes, of course I will marry you. I love you so much." The tears started flowing down her cheeks. She stood up with Roman, in unison, kissing and hugging each other in the middle of the restaurant.

There was loud applause, and both turned to see the waiters, hostess and other patrons clapping their hands.

Maya had come home. She had finally found what she had been looking for, right here, in Manhattan.